A Little Further Off

The Second Collection of Diverse Short Stories

Kenneth W. Hummell

FreeState LLC

With all my heart and being, I dedicate this book
to my late wife, Jo.

His Stories

His wife used to tell him
Both his stories and he
Were a little off
So, his book is for her
His writer friends
Are proud of him
And cheer him on
He's not out of stories yet
By H.R. Shavor

Table of Oddities

From the Shadows

Ken woke with a start, his mind filled with the vision of that hideous face. Stark white skin, egg-shaped head, large bulging blood-red eyes, and a huge oval-shaped mouth filled with sharp, finely pointed teeth. A shark's twin, with legs instead of fins. His mind seemed frozen on that horrific vision, then suddenly, the entire incident cascaded through his brain as if he was replaying the memory of those terrifying moments on fast-forward.

Ken remembered entering the butcher shop with his partner, Paul, and seeing a four-foot-tall, stark white midget with large red eyes and a huge mouth, wearing odd baggy, ill-fitting clothing. The figure brought to mind someone wearing a Halloween costume. The ugly midget was standing in the center of the room. Immediately, before Ken could even think about what was happening, the weird-looking figure launched itself through the air like a guided missile, impacted his chest, and knocked him to the floor. As it grabbed hold of him and bit him on the left shoulder, Ken managed to shoot it four times in the stomach. The bullets had absolutely no effect. It tore a mouthful of flesh and shirt from Ken's shoulder and calmly chewed.

Ken's response was to jam the barrel of his Berretta into the hideous creature's side and empty its magazine. But even after being shot by eight more rounds, the abomination didn't even flinch. It swallowed the first bite and was going back for seconds when Ken heard the roar of Paul's .44 Magnum. The nightmare creature's head exploded, covering Ken with a mist of blood, meat, bone, and brains. The speeding bullet only missing Ken's head by a narrow margin. Thank God Paul was an excellent shot.

The horrendous creature's muscles jerked erratically in spasms as death approached. Then the body became limp, and Ken rolled it off of him and onto the floor. He vaguely remembered Paul standing there with his revolver in hand, immobile, the gun still pointing in Ken's direction.

The last thing Ken remembered before slipping into pain-induced unconsciousness was Paul being attacked by at least four of the hideous creatures, each chomping on a different portion of Paul's anatomy. Paul blew another one's head off, then his revolver was ripped from his hand and his blood rained onto the floor as he fought for his life. His hideous screams reverberated through Ken's mind, becoming quieter and more distant, then total silence as Paul died and Ken lost consciousness!

Ken woke in a hospital bed with two men in suits watching him like he was one of the creatures that had bitten him. He struggled to sit up and yelled, "Paul! Paul! Where are you?"

One suit-clad individual stepped closer, put his hand on Ken's shoulder, and stated in a calm, quiet, reassuring voice, "He didn't make it, Ken. Take it easy, calm down, you're OK. That bite on your shoulder is healing fine and your collarbone was only partially bitten through. You'll be up and around in no time."

Ken laid back down and calmed himself. Then it hit him like a fast-moving semi-truck. Paul was really dead, eaten alive, by those hideous Fairies! He had watched while those vile creatures had munched Paul like a sandwich. He started talking so fast that even he couldn't understand what he was trying to say, realized what he was doing, and then forced himself to calm down again. He was finally able to ask, "Who saved me? How come, I'm still alive?"

The same suit sighed and then spoke. "The local police were notified of the gunshots coming from the butcher shop and arrived in time to save you from bleeding to death. The Fairies had already left the shop with Paul's body and their own dead. We think that they loaded them into a truck, but we aren't really sure. Evidently, they had decided to remove your body last, and because of that, you are here and still alive. The Fairies eluded the police, but they are still looking for them. After finding you, the police called us and an ambulance. You were brought to this hospital and were treated for a dog bite. Remember, this is very important: it was a Doberman that bit you! Don't ever forget that. We don't want the public to panic. You have been unconscious for three days and now we need you to tell us everything that you can remember."

Ken told the suits what he could recall in short spurts and between naps, including the Fairies' description. They finally left after they were forced to wake him up for the umpteenth time. In the days after, he saw no one but the hospital staff who cared for him. He lay in bed and thought over all he knew about those loathsome creatures, his memory returning to normal as time passed.

It had all started for him after a stint in the Army. He was invited to join a clandestine government group. Their mission was to pursue and eradicate a species of rampaging Fairies that consumed human flesh. At first, Ken thought that it was all a joke. Or some politician had gone bananas. Then he saw the proof and became very serious about his new task.

The government had discovered a depression, or hole in the floor of the southern Texas desert. The first indication of the Fairies' existence was in and around that hole. They started as extremely small, winged creatures with a life span measured in days who lived on fruit. When meat was introduced to their diet, by illegal immigrants sneaking into this country and falling into the hole, the Fairies' lifespans increased, as did their size, strength, and appetites.

After many generations, they managed to leave the hole and hunt in the surrounding desert where they fed upon human flesh and evolved. They lost their wings, gained mass and muscle, and became albinos. Their lifespan quickly extended, and presently they were managing to hide in the shadows of the human population and had spread throughout the United States. They consumed human flesh in order to satisfy their hunger and continue their rapid evolution. Ken and Paul's job was to hunt them down and kill them, while other teams were charged with the removal and disposal of the Fairies' remains.

Entering the butcher shop was their first mission and, of course, Paul's last! Ken spent three months in the hospital due to his bite becoming infected, and during that time he repeatedly promised himself: one, that he would track down and kill every damn Fairy in existence, and two, he was purchasing a .44 Magnum and a case of high-velocity hollow point ammunition ASAP.

The suits returned to talk to him on several occasions, and each time before leaving, they warned him to keep his mouth shut. They became upset when he asked them questions such as: "When Paul and I were being trained, why didn't they show us a picture, or at least inform us of what the Fairies had become?"

One of his other extremely pertinent unanswered questions was why had they not been informed to carry large caliber weapons instead of a 9mm pop gun and aim for the Fairies' heads? If Paul hadn't just happened to love his .44 Magnum and practice headshots, Ken would be dead! The suits usually pretended that they didn't hear his questions and then left hurriedly.

He finally received some answers and didn't like most of them. He was informed that the government had absolutely no idea that the Fairies had evolved so far. After all, it had taken a considerable amount of time to organize and train the response teams and convince the proper politicians that the Fairies even existed, let alone were dangerous enough to need eradication.

Then just over a year ago, the agents lost contact with the Fairies living in the desert outside the hole, and no one really knew how many generations that amount of time represented. Ken and Paul's unfortunate interaction with the Fairies had started new speculation and training procedures. All the new teams formed were updated with the pertinent facts.

On their last visit before Ken's release from the hospital, the suits informed him that his services were no longer required and that if he ever told anyone about anything having to do with the Fairies, he would be arrested and tossed in a prison somewhere, never to be heard from again. Ken lost his temper and vehemently pointed out that he was the only person alive who had seen the new

Fairy breed, and how stupid it was to fire him. He also stated that he had a strong idea of how they were hiding and feeding themselves, and he was not telling anyone unless he stayed on the payroll.

He was stretching things of course, but was desperate to keep his job! Hunting Fairies was time-consuming and expensive. With the government paying the bills he would go farther and eat much better. A no-income situation might force him to have to barbecue what he hunted. Uch!

He also stated that witnessing Paul's death furnished him a very personal reason to find and terminate the entire Fairy species, and motivation was always a large factor in how hard someone worked at any particular job. His last argument was that he was going to find and kill Fairies no matter what, whether or not he was a government employee, so they might as well keep him on the payroll.

Someone high up listened to his words and took

them to heart because not only was he rehired, he was promoted. After a short recovery time, some physical therapy, and a visit to a local gun shop to purchase a .44 Magnum and ammunition, he was given his new position. He became the leader of a group of ten men with an unlimited budget and one mission: kill Fairies, no matter what they looked like, or where they lived!

The first item on Ken's agenda was to start at the beginning and find out if any Fairies still lived in that desert area, and, if some did, what they had evolved into. The second item, of course, would be their termination. And absolutely the third would be removing the remaining Fairies from the rest of the country.

He was told that there were several hundred Fairies still living in the hole and that the government was supplying them with food, mostly beef. He visited and was appalled at what he found. The bottom of the hole was littered with the skeletal remains of all kinds of animals, including humans. The bones devoid of all meat, and their surfaces polished from being nibbled and licked. Not a single fruit tree lived or remained standing. The noxious smell of rotting skeletons wafting from the hole was enough to make anyone within a mile of the place sick to their stomach.

After observing the government agents forcing live cows over the edge of the hole, where they slid or rolled down a soft sand bank to the floor below, Ken threw up. Upon reaching the bottom, the cows were swarmed by starving Fairies who started devouring the pitiful animals one small mouthful at a time. The cows ran for their lives, mooing in mortal agony, until they were bitten so many times they bled to death. The scene caused the vision of Paul's death to explode in Ken's mind and spurred him to hate the Fairies even more.

Ken called his supervisor and obtained permission to eradicate the Fairies and their hole. Ken pointed out that on a regular basis a larger, wingless Fairy would crawl out of the hole and attack any living thing which happened to be present. If no one was there to witness the incidents or exactly how often they happened, who knew how many Fairies, which direction they went, what they looked like, or what happened to them. Evidently, evolution was still quite active in the Fairies' domain, even though they were mostly eating beef instead of human flesh.

Within hours, Ken obtained an Air Force bomber which dropped a very large white phosphorus bomb. The hole became much larger, deeper, and also devoid of all life! Ken laughed in joy, gave the hole the finger, and yelled, "Bite me!"

He ordered his crew to gear up, they had Fairies to hunt down and terminate. After Ken yelled "bite me" at the burning Fairy hole, the posse liked the wording so much that they adopted the phrase as their official greeting.

Ken and his crew started tracking the Fairies by going from town to town. They found and killed quite a few, enough at least to keep their boss happy and the money flowing. The scary portion of this hunt was that almost none of the terminated Fairies resembled each other, they had all evolved differently, or possibly, were from different generations. Only a Fairy or a scientist could know which version was true.

Homeless people and illegal immigrants seemed to be their favorite food. After all, no one misses either unless someone would notice and care about the fact that they didn't have to see or smell them anymore. Most of the US population would just thank God that they were gone.

A huge break came from out of the blue. In Los Angeles, California, the police recovered Paul's .44 Magnum, wristwatch, and cell phone. A citizen had purchased the revolver from a pawn shop, tried to register it, and the local police were notified about its former owner, Paul. When the police investigated the pawn shop, they found the watch and phone, and also that the shop was filled with hundreds of items for sale that the store had no record of where, or who, they had been obtained from.

Ken and crew arrived in Los Angeles two days later and went to the pawn shop immediately. The pawn shop manager was a young well-endowed woman dressed like a hooker, her mini skirt so short that her panties were visible, and her low-cut blouse barely covering her nipples. She refused to talk, told them to contact her attorney, then just stood and stared at them with a scowl on her face. Ken had her taken into custody and secured a local female cop to replace her as the store's manager. The replacement told anyone who asked that the former manager had fallen ill and was in the hospital.

In the storage room of the pawn shop, Ken found cartons and cartons of items that were obviously the personal effects of homeless people and illegals. Both categories were known to keep a few family heirlooms to remember their former lives, and the Fairies were selling them at a one hundred percent profit. In the pawn shop's refrigerator and at the manager's apartment, Ken's crew found human flesh sandwiches.

After a DNA test proved that the manager was human and not an evolved Fairy, a ton of questions were raised about why a human would become a cannibal for no apparent reason. The manager still refused to talk, and Ken wondered if the answer was simply free meat, or possibly an acquired taste, or for that matter, a combination of both. It was obvious that she had a dire mental problem or she wouldn't touch, let alone eat, human meat.

It was eight days before the Fairies delivered another load of items for the shop to sell, and Ken and crew received an eye-opening surprise. The Fairy deliveryman looked almost human unless you looked very closely. He was five-foot-five inches tall and extremely strong, tossing the heavy boxes around like they weighed nothing. He was dressed in very baggy clothes to mask his odd build and almost never opened his mouth. When he talked, he mumbled, keeping his lips almost sealed.

After shooting him in the head it became evident that the only thing that hadn't evolved were his teeth, and probably his lust for human flesh. Evidently, the Fairies were continuing on their evolutionary trip into the future.

After checking the pawn shop's tax records, Ken found out that it was part of a large corporation that owned many various businesses spread out across the country including six more pawn shops, five butcher shops, a trucking company, a fertilizer manufacturing plant, ten restaurants, and fifty lawn service companies. Ken's brain clicked. What he was thinking scared the hell out of him. Sometimes it paid to have an active imagination. His was very active and formed a very plausible but frightening Fairy agenda: kidnap and kill the homeless and illegals, own pawn shops to sell anything of value recovered from the victims, own a trucking company to distribute the bodies and personal effects to the appropriate locations for processing or sale, own butcher shops to cut up the bodies, own a fertilizer plant to grind the bones, skin, and skulls into an organic mulch, own numerous lawn service companies to disperse that mulch, and own restaurants to sell the meat that you don't need for Fairy consumption.

After all, who would eat a delicious soup, stew, meatloaf, or even a steak, and dream that it was human flesh. All any normal person would think about was if the meat was tasty or not and if it was worth the price they were being charged. This was called, in Ken's opinion, how to hide in the shadows of normal human lifestyles and make millions of dollars while doing it.

Now all Ken had to do was convince his superior so that he and his men could hunt down and kill them all, both human collaborators and Fairies! That was Ken and his men's opinion, but Ken's superior had to give his permission on that one very important question. Should we eliminate the humans that were colluding with the Fairies? His superior's answer was no surprise. He agreed with Ken and company, yes, definitely kill them, why wouldn't we? They're cannibals!

Ken took care of the hooker-look-alike, cannibalistic pawn shop manager personally. His disposal team complained about having to remove a human body, so Ken told them that he would handle her removal this time, but they had better get used to it. There would be many more.

On her way to work, the manager accidentally stepped out in front of a garbage truck and was run over, her head smashed flatter than a pancake. Ken was the only witness and informed the local cops that it wasn't the truck driver's fault. The hooker was staggering as if she was high or drunk, tripped over her own feet, and fell into the street just as the truck passed. The needle marks on her arms convinced the cops and the case was forgotten. Another hooker drug addict bit the dust.

The government used local ordinances and tax levies to shut down and confiscate the pawn shop, making it look like normal city business. You know, the city needs money, and they are going to get it anyway, and from anyone, they can! Ken and crew moved on to other portions of the massive corporation.

The posse, as Ken referred to himself and his men, wanted to start at the top, at corporate headquarters, but the higher powers told them absolutely not. At the time, their reasoning seemed valid. But later on, the real reason surfaced. Their argument was that if the Fairies' leaders were removed, the remaining Fairies would scatter, making it difficult, or impossible, to find and eliminate them. They ordered the posse to start at the bottom, take their time, and do it right, with the major emphasis on *take your time*. After discussing their superior's decision, the entire posse agreed.

They managed to locate and eliminate several hundred Fairies and their human helpers over the next year, and the only complaint they received was from the team responsible for removing and disposing of the bodies. They wanted the posse to take a long vacation because making bodies disappear was getting tiresome.

Everyone noted one very unusual aspect of the Fairies' human cohorts, they were almost always young females dressed like hookers. The posse surmised that the Fairies liked to admire the female human form since they themselves all looked the same: muscular and ugly. The posse just called them all "he" because it was impossible to tell which sex they were until they were dead and could be examined closely. No one from the posse felt comfortable doing a sexual examination; they just inserted their fingers in the bullet holes and bragged about how great a shot they were, then stuck to the title of "he."

The Fairies were appearing more human-like as

they evolved but still muscle-bound and demonic looking. And the corporation was hiring much more adept attorneys to fight the loss of their local businesses. Then another wrinkle! While raiding a butcher shop in Kansas, the posse discovered that the Fairy manager had shacked up with a human woman and had two half-breed children.

During the investigation, no human meat was found in the family's home, only the butcher shop. Ken personally checked the kid's teeth and found them slightly pointy but still almost human. The kids were, to be as polite as possible, never going to win any beauty contests, but at least they could become professional wrestlers or any other occupation that depended on muscle, as both kids had more than their fair share. No one in the posse wanted to kill a mother and her two offspring no matter how much they hated the Fairies, so Ken made an executive decision.

Instead of using the government's body removal and disposal team, he did them another favor.

He faked the Fairy father's death to look like an accident by blowing the entire shop and its staff of Fairy butchers to smithereens with an explosion caused by an unfortunate major gas leak and twenty propane tanks dispersed throughout the shop. The bodies were too badly injured and burned for the coroner to notice that each one had a huge bullet hole in its head. Then Ken neglected to inform his superior about the mom and her two kids, and the entire posse agreed to protect the family at all costs by never telling a soul about their existence!

After losing almost half of the corporate-owned companies, the corporation sent Fairies to kill the posse. They were waiting at the fertilizer plant, the next posse attack point. Evidently, someone in the know had sold out Ken and company. The Fairies lost the battle. When teeth go up against guns, the teeth almost always lose, especially when the guns are very large caliber, and the shooters are experts. Later, it was learned that some politicians had decided that the Fairies could be useful and had financed the corporation's start-up. They thought the Fairies could serve the greater good! The removal of the homeless and illegals would save the entire government from city to state and, above all, the feds billions of dollars per year.

The Fairies and their politician buddies found that doing away with the posse was no easy matter, although they kept trying, wounding several, but killing none. The powers to be set numerous traps for the posse, and each time the Fairies involved became corpses. The posse laughed when Ken quipped that the Fairy traps for the posse made it much easier and faster to find and kill Fairies than the posse's usual methods. It didn't take long for Ken to figure out that it was his own leaders, not some faraway politicians, who wanted the posse dead. He set a trap of his own by inviting his immediate superior to meet him in person to discuss who was leaking information to the Fairies.

Ken told him when and where the posse was going to strike the Fairies next and invited him to accompany them. When the posse arrived at the location, the superior suddenly decided to wait in the van since he only packed a 9mm Glock. Ken and crew entered and killed every Fairy in the building.

The Fairies had laid a decent trap, but the posse decimated them anyway. Again, teeth and muscle were no match for large caliber weapons. Then the posse waited. Within minutes of the ending of the gunfire, the posse's own superior strolled in and yelled for the Fairies to come out and thank him. Ken thanked him personally by shooting him in the genitals with a 160-grain hollow point bullet from his .44 Magnum. Then the entire posse huddled around their bleeding, critically injured supervisor, and listened to him confess all.

He gave up everyone involved between bouts of pleading to be taken to a hospital and crying for his mommy. He named names, addresses, and phone numbers and, in several cases, even politician's mistresses. He didn't shut up until he finally bled to death, which took almost forty-five minutes. The posse immediately made plans to kill everyone named and get it accomplished before being eliminated themselves.

The politicians' plans were twofold: use the Fairies to lower the homeless and illegal immigrant populations discreetly, thereby saving many dollars for the government, plus, the corporation made millions of dollars in profit each year, divided equally between the politicians' personal bank accounts, and then, in case the public ever discovered what was happening, the posse killing the Fairies would make it look like the government was trying to eliminate the problem. The plan had worked well until the posse proved how adept they were at tracking and terminating the Fairies.

This two-pronged approach wouldn't make much sense to most people, and the government would skate once again. Kind of like Vietnam, the government enters the war for the benefit of a few politicians, drafts men and forces them to go fight, then blames the men for the war's length and treats them like garbage! The politicians came out smelling like roses instead of shit like they really deserved.

Before bleeding to death, the posse's supervisor also disclosed that a secret dinner meeting involving almost all the upper echelons of this Fairy plot was about to happen and where it was going to be held. The posse immediately formulated a plan and implemented it, after all, what goes around comes around, at least with a little help from the posse.

They arrived during the set up for the dinner and posed as food workers and deliverymen. A Fairy meat truck was parked out back of the kitchen, and portions of human bodies were brought inside and stored in the walk-in freezer. All meat served at the dinner was human flesh.

When the meal was about half consumed, Ken

and crew had a local cop call his division and report that a large party of wealthy cannibals was consuming human flesh and in possession of human corpses, which the cop had personally witnessed and had photographic evidence as proof. The posse then left the premises quickly. The local police raided the dinner and discovered the human remains in the truck, the freezer, and the kitchen.

Everyone at the dinner, including the kitchen staff, was arrested. Later, when the police tested the meat served and found it to be human, all the dinner guests and restaurant staff were found guilty of murder and the consumption of human flesh. They were sentenced to thirty years in prison and the judge decreed that they were to be served only a vegan diet. The defense attorney filed an appeal because, according to him, serving vegan food to a cannibal would be cruel and inhuman punishment. The same judge threw the appeal out of court and filed a complaint against the attorney.

The corporation dissolved. Ken's posse spent the next three years hunting and killing Fairies, their cohorts, and the remaining politicians and government suck-asses that still lived. They lost count when the deceased numbered over three thousand. After several months of not being able to find a single Fairy, the posse was transferred to the FBI. Ken stayed for six months then resigned. He thought that the FBI's name should be changed to the Federal Bureau of Imbeciles because no one ever seemed to do anything except cover up for politicians or sit around bragging to each other about how great they were.

Ken returned to his hometown of Fresno, California, and became a successful private detective working for corporations and wealthy people across the country. Randomly, he would also remove a Fairy that he found hiding somewhere. Of course, not having a body disposal team, they were always accidental deaths. The remaining few were almost indistinguishable from humans, but he usually found them by the high rate of missing people in a certain area and singled them out by their mouthful of very pointy teeth. Luckily, there weren't many left alive, but those who still lived still loved human meat!

I realize that after reading about the existence of Fairies and their love of human flesh, you will be very alert. Keep an eye out for their pointy teeth and take my advice. If you listen to me, you will be much happier!

Behave yourself, but if you can't, misbehave doing something that you really really enjoy! Because if you don't, you're just wasting your time. Remember, Fairies could pop out of the shadows and eat you anytime or anywhere! And oh yeah, don't forget, your government might just be helping them!

Aw, Rats!

"This living in a tent sucks. Boy, am I cold and damp." Tracy snuggled down into the pile of assorted dirty clothing he was using as a mattress and continued bitching softly to himself.

"Just think, a little less than a year ago, I was still in the army and thought my life was so bad I was thinking about deserting. I stuck it out long enough to get my honorable discharge, but being a Vietnam veteran, no one will hire me. Now I live in a garbage-strewn alley, in a leaky, worn-out canvass tent with no heat or mattress, and am forced to scrub floors in the local strip joint for next to nothing. Sure makes army life seem more tolerable."

Tracy stopped talking and stared off into space for several minutes, a blank look on his face, then blurted loudly, "Listen to me, I'm talking like an idiot! The army is definitely not good enough for me to even think about re-enlisting. Army life makes this alley look good. Now my day-to-day existence might be akin to living in a garbage dump, but being back in the army would be like swimming in a septic tank full of turds. Plain shitty! Just imagining being forced to take orders from those incompetent, affirmative-action assholes again is enough to make me sick. So, grow up, pussy. Things will get better eventually, and if they don't, there's always suicide.

"Think! Be unique. Do it somewhere public. In the center of a crowd. Make a huge bloody mess and cause every on-looker that sees it happen to throw up. Just thinking about the poor slobs that would have to clean up all the vomit, blood, ground meat, and bone makes me feel so much better. Because I sure as hell wouldn't be around to be one of the cleaning crew."

After another spell of staring off into the distance, Tracy screamed, "Why don't you shut up? I'm not a chickenshit. I would definitely shoot some asshole that messed with me then stick my finger in the bullet hole and wiggle it, but I'm never killing myself, especially with a bomb. How deranged would a person have to be? I'm nutty enough to imagine it, but not nearly nutty enough to do it!"

He finally fell asleep and slept through most of the day. He woke just in time to walk to work, his stomach growling from hunger. He arrived at the club, snuck into the kitchen, and helped himself to some food from the refrigerator. Luckily for Tracy, his boss's mouth ran constantly, at maximum volume, and always heralded his arrival. Tracy slipped out the rear door unnoticed and traversed the building, managing to finish eating his stolen food before re-entering the club through the front entrance as if he were just arriving.

The owner was standing in the middle of the bar yelling at the top of his lungs about some ungrateful bastard stealing from him, and that he was planning to fire whoever it was just before they received a lengthy prison term. Tracy was about to admit his guilt when a cop walked in and stated loudly, "I hate to interrupt the temper tantrum, Bud, but it would be nice to know which register was rifled and how much money was stolen?"

Tracy breathed a huge sigh of relief. It wasn't about stolen food, but money. The owner grabbed the cop by the arm and dragged him to the end of the bar. He pointed at the cash register and stated in a vile tone, "There, idiot, how many registers do you see? You going to take fingerprints? Of course not. You have no supplies with you. You're just putting on a show. And for your information, we have no idea the amount of money stolen. The receipts haven't been totaled yet, but the register always starts with five hundred dollars in assorted bills and change. So the dollar amount has to be more than that! Now! Would you mind actually doing something, or do I need to call the idiotic, fat loafer in charge?"

As the cop started scrutinizing the register, the owner turned and screamed at his gawking employees, "Listen, you worthless pieces of shit, get your asses to work! I don't pay you to stand around and stare. And you, Arnold, don't just stand there playing with yourself! Get to work!"

All employees present dispersed quickly. The police officer turned and started to say something, but Tracy didn't stick around to listen. He needed his job, so he headed for the cleaning closet to get his mop and broom. The cop looked pissed off, and besides, the barroom floor looked like a pigpen, including certain globs of something which looked and smelled like shit, but was probably some expensive Vietnamese cuisine from the club's kitchen which a patron had tasted and then tossed.

The one outstanding quality of Vietnamese food was that it tasted so foul, even when it was prepared properly, that most Americans couldn't tell the difference between quality and crap. Liquor was about the only substance that could remove its foul taste, hence the reason to sell it in a bar. This club's minimum-wage Vietnamese chef's creations made crap look and smell good.

The police officer left after about fifteen minutes and it took Tracy several more hours to clean up the barroom. He was barely finished before it was time to open. The rest of the night was normal—crappy. Some drunk would spill their drink, up-chuck, throw a bottle at someone and smash it, or piss themselves, and Tracy had to clean up the mess. The bathrooms were the worst. Probably half of the men missed the urinals, and a large percentage of both men and women missed the toilets, and not always while throwing up. Tracy could never imagine how someone could take a crap on the floor right beside a commode, but it happened quite often, and, every once in a while, someone even took one on the floor, in the corner of the bathroom. Tracy reached the conclusion that the corner users were the more sober ones who couldn't stand to use the nasty stalls. Either way, he was the one who had to clean up the mess no matter what, where, or by whom it had been deposited.

The next morning, as Tracy was leaving the club, the owner handed him a twenty-dollar bill, and before Tracy could complain, snarled, "I had money stolen from my business and everyone takes a pay cut until I get my funds back. Your contribution is twenty bucks a night, and if you don't like it, there are plenty of homeless, worthless, assholes out there besides you that need cash. I can always find another one. Take it or leave it."

Tracy took it. After all, he was starving. He purchased a pizza and a bottle of beer for nineteen dollars and ninety-nine cents and wandered back to his alley paradise to sit in his mansion and enjoy his feast. Halfway through his meal, his imagination died and he looked around and whined, "Look at this dump! What makes my life even worth living?

"Maybe, I should rob the club, or at least kick the shit out of its loudmouthed backstabbing owner. If I were lucky, a cop would shoot me and put me out of my misery. Or I would get caught and put in jail. Food, a roof, and a bed. Damn right better than starving, or freezing to death in this filthy alley."

A long, drawn-out pause, then a short burst of laughter followed by a deep breath, and in a stern voice Tracy stated, "Of course, I am forgetting Bubba. With my luck, he would be my cellmate, beat the hell out of me, steal my food, and overuse my poor asshole. He scares me shitless. Thanks to my Bubba nightmares, this alley is looking much better."

Before he could continue his rant, Tracy's attention was diverted from his absolutely moronic thoughts and words to a large gray animal crawling into his tent. At first, he thought it was a big cat, or maybe a possum, but after studying it, he realized that it was actually a huge rat with a broken rear leg. Tracy started to stomp on its head with his boot, but as he was positioning his body to enable himself to use a more powerful downward stroke, the rat looked up at him with the most soft, pleading, gentle, intelligent, blue eyes that Tracy had ever seen. Tracy melted like an ice cube in a microwave set on high! Within an hour the rat's leg was splinted, he had eaten his fill of pizza, and was snuggled against Tracy's back where he would stay warm. The only problem was the rat's aroma, which was making Tracy sick to his stomach.

It was several weeks before the rat, now named

Pete, could walk properly. Tracy really enjoyed having a friend. Pete always listened intently to every word that came out of Tracy's mouth, of which there were many, never interrupted or complained, and was almost always waiting in the tent for Tracy to arrive home. Pete was the largest, and only blue-eyed, gray rat that Tracy had ever seen and seemed to be so intelligent at times that he was almost scary. On the downside, Pete smelled like shit. After all, he crawled around in the city sewer system, and since they were sharing the tent and sleeping on the same pile of old clothes, Tracy started hauling water home to give Pete a bath, which Pete learned to do for himself and loved almost as much as pizza.

One morning when Tracy arrived back at the tent, Pete was waiting for him with presents. A cell phone, a diamond ring, a silver necklace with turquoise settings, and a Colt revolver. Tracy examined the items, except the gun, which he wrapped very carefully in an old t-shirt. He remarked, "Pete, I know you can't answer me, but I sure wish you could. Where in the hell did you get this stuff? How come it's all so clean, except the gun, and how did you ever get it all home?"

Instantly, Pete, in a very whispery-sounding voice answered, "The sewers, Tracy. I got them out of the sewer pipes, and it took me several trips and a used plastic bag to get them here. I washed everything clean, but the gun, in the gutter across the street."

To say Tracy was frozen with amazement would be an understatement. For several minutes Tracy stared at Pete, trying to decide whether to stay or run. Then he burst into laughter. Shaking his head, he muttered, "I have to quit talking to myself and a rat, or I'm going to be as crazy as a loon. If I'm not already!"

Pete interjected. "Tracy, I learned to talk by listening to people, mostly you, and then practicing. Why are you going to go crazy?"

Tracy hesitated and patted Pete's head, then

grabbed him roughly and hoisted him high enough to where he could look Pete directly in the face. He ordered, "Pete, say something. Say something, now! I want to see your lips move."

And Pete's lips moved. "Tracy, please put me down before I bite you. You're hurting me."

Tracy immediately placed Pete gently on the floor and put both his hands on his own forehead exclaiming, "Well, my head's not hot, so I'm not suffering from a fever. Guess I'm just fucking crazy!"

Pete erupted with a short, shrill giggle and then stated, "Tracy, cut it out. You're not crazy. I can talk. You are my friend. I brought this stuff here to show that. Now stop messing around, say hello, tell me if you like what I brought, and if we can trade this stuff for some pizza. Also, would you like me to bring more?"

Tracy swallowed hard, slowly shook his head, and then exclaimed loudly, "Shit!"

He thought things over for several minutes,

took a deep breath, and then continued quite calmly, "Hi, Pete. I think I can get enough money out of what you brought to buy us pizza, and yes, we can always use more items. The gun will be tricky. I do have an idea, but I'll need to know exactly where it came from, and I am very sorry that I hurt you. I hope that you know that I would never do that intentionally. Hey Pete, it's your turn to talk now, so say something."

"OK, Tracy, You don't have to tell me when to talk, believe me, I know. I'm not stupid. You might have to tell me to shut up once in a while though. Ha, ha. Yes, I can get lots more stuff. The sewers are full of all kinds of debris. The gun came from the southeast corner of Fifth Street and Uvalde. By the way, what's money? You have never mentioned that word before."

It took Tracy considerable time to explain to Pete what money was and what it was used for. Of course, a sizeable portion of that time was consumed by Tracy silently staring at Pete in absolute awe. They finally agreed that Pete would trade the sewer items to Tracy for pizza and anything else he needed, and Tracy would worry about the money aspects of their deal. After all, a talking, big, blue-eyed rat with a smelly plastic bag full of cash would attract a lot of attention, and if Pete didn't want to find himself locked in a cage in some government laboratory, he would be extremely careful who saw him and whom he talked to.

Tracy spent the rest of the day visiting numerous pawnshops until he finally found one that didn't cTracy consumed a sizeable portion of that timeare where the items to be pawned originated. The amount of money Tracy received for Pete's gifts was so much more than Tracy expected that he pondered quitting his job at the club, but then had second thoughts. What would happen long-term if Pete couldn't live up to his portion of their deal?

Short-term Pete did, and Tracy and Pete ate

pizza three times a day every day. Tracy even purchased a new tent, an air mattress, and a battery-powered heater. He also leased a water tank to be placed in the alley and filled weekly. Water was an absolute necessity for removing the crap from both Pete and his donations. The clean-up was the biggest and nastiest problem with their arrangement. It made cleaning the bathrooms at the club look and smell good. Luckily, all the shit-covered plastic bags fit into the dumpster at the other end of the alley and the breeze blew from the tent to the dumpster, wafting the nasty fumes away.

Tracy opened a savings account at a local bank branch, although the bank manager hesitated when he found out where and how Tracy was living, but changed his mind when Tracy flashed some cash. The bank did, however, refuse to open a checking account due to the lack of a proper address.

Pete brought two more handguns home and

Tracy was finally forced to implement his plan. Luckily, Pete was afraid of guns and had not washed any of them. Tracy informed Pete to never wash any knives or guns, ever, and explained what fingerprints were and how they could be used. The entire time Pete kept looking at his hairy paws and asking some of the most stupid questions imaginable. Tracy, in desperation, finally screamed, "Pete, enough is enough! Shut up and listen to me. Don't wash any weapons, it will make them worthless."

Pete finally nodded yes, but Tracy could tell he still wanted more answers. Tracy left immediately to deliver the days' worth of items to the pawnshop and drop off a bank deposit. Then he wandered around the neighborhood for the rest of the day to avoid Pete and his stupid questions.

One of the police officers who patrolled the strip joint where Tracy worked was very friendly. Tracy showed him the first gun and explained that he had found it in the city sewer and the exact location where it was found. The cop accepted the gun and thanked Tracy while at the same time holding his nose. Several days later, he informed Tracy that ballistics had proven the gun was a murder weapon and that fingerprints were obtained from it. The killer was arrested because of his prints on the gun and its bullets and confessed almost immediately. No lawyers and no trial equals quick and cheap justice.

The cop handed Tracy two hundred dollars then jokingly remarked, "Tracy, if you find any more smelly weapons, give them to me and I'll make you my confidential informant. If you do, I can pay you."

The next night Tracy gave the cop two more pistols and a bloody knife along with the explicit positions at which they were obtained. This time the cop wasn't laughing when he looked at Tracy and remarked, "You have got to be kidding me! How do you get down into those sewer pipes? You'd have to crawl."

Tracy quipped, "I pretend to be a turd, officer, and flush myself. That's really easy when you are as full of shit as I am."

The police officer shook his head slowly no, and then stated firmly, "These weapons are no joking matter, Tracy. Get serious!"

Tracy answered quickly, using an even firmer tone than the cop's. "Don't look a gift turd in the mouth, officer. I can always find another cop to give them to. Although, I guess at two hundred bucks apiece they're not really gifts, are they?"

The police officer spoke very slowly as if he was thinking over each word. "OK, let's not go crazy. We need each other. You are as of this minute, my informant. All right with you, Tracy?"

Tracy nodded and the deal was done, his plan finally implemented. There is nothing quite as satisfying as obtaining money from government assholes instead of being forced to give it to them.

Tracy received confidential informant money weekly, even when he furnished no weapons. He talked it over with Pete and they decided to tell the strip club owner where to shove it. As Tracy was leaving the club after doing so, the bartender informed him that the club's robbery had been solved. It was the owner's son and he had been arrested.

Tracy couldn't help himself, he returned to his former boss and demanded the rest of his pay, and when the asshole refused, Tracy ridiculed him and his son. "In your family's case, the phrase 'an apple doesn't fall far from its tree' should not be used. However, my rendition 'a turd doesn't fall far from its asshole' is more than appropriate."

The sleazy asshole had a bouncer physically toss Tracy out into the alley. Tracy decided that the cuts and bruises he received from his forced ejection were more than worth the sick angry look on the owner's face, but the wages Tracy had been cheated out of were another matter completely. Tracy promised himself that in the future he would figure out a way for Pete and company to get even for him.

Pete upped the quantity of sewer items by recruiting more rats. He was the only one who could talk to Tracy but interpreted between his crew and Tracy quite adequately. Pete's crew all delivered items to the alley, and soon the tent wasn't large enough to house Pete and Tracy along with the items that Pete's minions acquired, not to mention the number of pizzas necessary to feed all involved. Other problems also arose. The dumpster was overflowing with empty pizza boxes and nasty plastic bags, and the water tank needed to be replaced with a larger unit. Tracy was looking for someplace to rent when fate knocked on his tent.

A local Mexican gang dispatched one of their members to intimidate Tracy into paying them protection money. They had become aware of his visits to the pawnshop and wanted their cut of Tracy and Pete's proceeds. Every business in the area coughed up dollars to the gang or suffered violent consequences. After Tracy laughed in the gangbanger's face, the badass made the mistake of punching Tracy in the nose and then threatening him with a knife.

Tracy lost his temper and was in the process of breaking the asshole's neck when, from out of nowhere, a pack of rats attacked, biting the gangbanger. One rat tore out his jugular vein, scratching Tracy's left arm severely, which happened to be wrapped around the banger's neck. Several others removed the banger's genitals. The rest munched on any portion of the dumb ass's anatomy that they could reach. The idiot was dead in seconds.

After Tracy bandaged his arm, he and Pete argued over which came first, death by broken neck, or by rat bite. Pete almost collapsed from laughing so hard when Tracy remarked, "Before I order the pizzas, Pete, maybe you should ask your crew: after this *raw* appetizer, would they like to switch from pizzas to burritos? There is a great

Mexican restaurant three blocks south, of course, everything they sell is well done, not *raw*."

Several more minutes of joking were followed by the sudden arrival of reality. A bloody dead body lying in the alley in front of their tent was definitely not a laughing matter. Pete pointed out to Tracy that at least he was safe, after all, it was obvious that the banger had died from rat bites. Tracy was still scared out of his wits!

All his imagining aside, he really didn't want to go to prison, especially now, with money in the bank, a friend, and possibly even a future. And of course, nightmares about Bubba still terrified him. He panicked, guzzled an entire bottle of tequila, and passed out. The next morning when Tracy woke up, his head throbbed and his vision was blurry, but it was evident that the body was gone, and a horde of bloodstained fat rats were lying packed tightly all over the tent's floor. Pete finally awakened and explained. He and his crew had spent most of the night chewing the body up into pieces, swallowing most of the flesh, and carrying the rest into the sewer system. The nasty job would have been accomplished sooner but the skull and large bones presented a major time-consuming obstacle.

Pete's last comment was undeniably epic. "What goes into the sewer system, stays in the sewer system. Unless Pete and company decide it is worth some money and should be retrieved."

Tracy quipped, "That gangbanger was definitely a piece of shit, dead or alive, and I will be eternally grateful for Pete thinking of how to remove his body and Pete's friends for eating and flushing it. Now let's get you guys a bath, the blood cleaned up, and order some pizzas."

The illegal, despicable gang upped the ante, and this time they sent three mean-looking dipshits, all armed. Pete and his rat army chewed them up and spit them out, literally. This time, Tracy helped his friends by smashing the skulls and the larger bones into small pieces with a hammer. The banger's weapons were delivered to the cop who was, as usual, grateful. Tracy and Pete talked things over and decided to dispatch scouts to find the gang's location and put a number to their membership. Upon the scouts' return, plans were devised.

Tracy and Pete pondered their situation and decided the smart thing to do was attack instead of waiting to be ambushed. The gang occupied an entire four-story abandoned building and consisted of only twenty members, which intrigued Tracy. This could be the solution to his and Pete's problems and the next step in their business's evolution.

Pete rounded up more help and informed Tracy that he needed at least sixty large pizzas to pay for their army. Tracy asked Pete how many rats were invited, and Pete laughed and stated, "Enough to remove all evidence of those illegal assholes existence."

When Tracy pressed the question, Pete finally admitted, "I'm not really sure, but I would guess that it's about five hundred, give or take a few."

The gang's removal happened the next day. Luckily, the building had a direct opening into the sewer system in its basement. After entering through the basement, Pete opened the front door for Tracy who had never seen that many rats in his life. Being mostly night stalkers and arrogant enough not to post guards, the gang members were all asleep or drunk, but several of the bangers still got off a shot or two. Otherwise, they all died quickly screaming their heads off. Being eaten and chewed apart while alive was evidently very traumatic and painful. Several rats were injured, but happily, none fatally. After the short altercation was over, the cleanup took the rest of the day and part of the following night. Tracy and his hammer really got a workout, as did the building's sewer pipe.

Tracy had the pizzas delivered just before midnight and after watching the rats devour their food, he remarked to Pete, "Do you realize that rats eat like pigs?"

Pete's answer sounded a little perturbed. "None of us rats has ever seen a pig, so maybe whatever a pig is, it eats like a rat. How come you're not eating at all, Tracy? Afraid that we rats will think you eat like a pig?"

Tracy didn't answer. Between watching the consumption and destruction of twenty bodies and then watching the rats consume pizza, he was having trouble keeping himself from throwing up, which seemed to be happening a lot lately. When he insisted that the bloody mess had to be cleaned up immaculately, Pete questioned his motives. Tracy stood and gestured around the room then asked, "Pete, how do you like our new home?"

Pete answered so quickly his first words almost drowned out Tracy's last word. "Damn, you're smart, Tracy! But how do we keep people from noticing? We don't exactly look like foreign gangbangers."

Tracy's answer startled both Pete and himself.

"We get ourselves a lawyer and buy the building, Pete. Your entire crew can move in with us. No one will ever see them, after all, they have their own private entrance in the basement, and the first floor will become our own pawnshop. Cut out the middleman. Sooner or later, the sewers will run out of items. Common sense says that they have to at some point. This way we will take legitimate pawns also."

Within six months The Pack Rats Pawnshop was up and running, helped through the political bullshit of acquiring a license by the police commissioner himself. Tracy gave the cop the fifteen guns and ten knives obtained from the gang and said that he found them all in a dumpster and furnished the address. The guns and knives were almost all linked to various crimes or criminals, and the cop didn't ask many questions. He just gave Tracy a five-hundred-dollar bonus and ignored the glaring question of where the astronomical number of items for sale at the pawnshop came from. He had just received a promotion because of the weapons, supplied by Tracy, solving so many crimes, and therefore, was planning to take very good care of Tracy and his business.

Local citizens kept showing up at the building to try to pay the gang their weekly protection money. Tracy kept telling them that the gang left town and that all the local businesses were safe and didn't have to pay anymore. Most hugged him or shook his hand and several women even tried to kiss him, but all involved thanked him. Most thought Tracy's explanation was pure bullshit, but didn't care as long as the gang was gone.

Business was extremely good, and Pete and Tracy thrived. They purchased several other abandoned buildings and hired the homeless to renovate and staff them. Of course, all the basements were turned into living quarters for Pete's ever-growing gang of rodents. Pete surprised Tracy by designing rat toilets and baths.

The toilets had a flushable tank covered with wire mesh. The mesh allowed the rat's turds to fall into the tank which then flushed automatically every day. The baths were shallow gutters filled with running water. The combination made the basements much easier to keep clean and more aromatic. Tracy never stopped congratulating Pete for his intelligence.

The local pizza joints delivered every day and the rats never complained about their food, although, every once in a while, a group of rats would get into a fight over the last piece, and one extremely nasty rat was executed for trying to horde an entire pizza.

Tracy's former employer's club was overrun by rodents several times, and the city health department finally closed it down. Tracy and Pete bought it for an astoundingly cheap price after the old owner tried to exterminate the pests on numerous occasions. It was almost as if the rats knew when the exterminators were going to dispense the poison and what rat traps were and where they were located.

The owner swore that Tracy had something to do with his rodent problem and mentioned it to the local paper, owned by the club owner's brother, who printed a very strange story about Tracy and his supposed abilities. It mentioned that numerous citizens had reported that items that they had lost down the sewers had been seen for sale in The Pack Rats Pawnshop. They also pointed out the name of Tracy's business, hinting that somehow Tracy had an in with the city's rat population.

Tracy sued for libel and won a huge settlement, bankrupting both the club owner and his brother. After all, how stupid could a person be to think that another human being could actually control vermin? Now Tracy and Pete owned a newspaper and strip club along with their other holdings. Tracy immediately switched the club's menu from Vietnamese to a different cuisine, pizza. He and Pete were the local pizza joints' superheroes.

Pete, who was getting rather old for a rat, laughed himself silly and told Tracy that he owed him big time for instigating his revenge. Tracy pointed out that he and Pete were partners, and, as such, shared in all the proceeds and even quoted how much money they had gained.

Pete's comeback was that he was the one who had to stay in hiding while Tracy could run around in public and enjoy himself. Tracy's last comment, "It's not my fault that I was born a human and you a rat. But you do have to admit that we make a good team," brought tears to Pete's blue eyes as he nodded his furry head in agreement.

Another gang tried to move into the neighborhood and mysteriously disappeared. That little trick cost Tracy and Pete another sixty pizzas, a bonus actually, since Tracy and Pete were already feeding almost every rat in town. At least another homeless man volunteered to man the hammer for a hundred bucks and a set of new clothes, which Tracy was more than willing to pay.

After this episode, Tracy and Pete had a serious talk about their future plans, and Tracy had to admit that he was worried about his existence without his partner and friend. Pete made Tracy's day by introducing him to his six-week-old sons, all four of whom had blue eyes and were learning to speak English.

Tracy fondled them and then commented, "Boy, are they big. At six weeks they are already half your size, Pete. By the time they grow up, I bet they weigh sixty pounds apiece."

Pete laughed and then quipped, "Tracy, you should see my other kids. I have so many I have lost count. The females love my blue eyes and we get together all the time, plus, unlike humans, we have multiple babies with each pregnancy. One of these days, my descendants might be the ones walking around in public, and your descendants might be the ones hiding in the basement."

Tracy felt obligated to point out that Pete was enjoying an awful lot of sex while in hiding, and he was getting very little. "Who knows, maybe my descendants would like to hide!"

Most people don't realize that a rat's paw is very similar to a human hand, and that they are also highly intelligent. Give them more size, add a vocabulary, and things might change. Who knows what, or how much. Only time will tell! Evolution is ongoing and tricky.

Desperate is Dangerous

Andy Donovan crawled slowly from his most treasured possession and home, a whirlpool refrigerator carton. He groaned with pain as he propped himself against the front of his pantry, a restaurant dumpster. The temperature had dipped below freezing the night before, and as the sun rose, the small amount of sunshine that managed to penetrate the alley's shadows warmed his spirit, if not his body. His stomach rumbled and rolled, but he had long ago found that hunger could be ignored for a considerable time, and as usual, he overrode his concerns about today's survival by retreating into his past. His fondest memories marched through his mind with the precision of a Green Beret Team which, for twenty-five years, he had led with such arrogance. He sat statue-like, his mind reliving his youth.

Reality returned, heralded by the blare of a horn followed by a shrill voice. "Get out of the way, ya' old bum!"

Andy's daydreams vanished like the dark before a sunrise. A truck was speeding down the alley. Its driver flipped Andy the finger and screamed, "I said, get out of the way or I'll run ya over!"

Andy unemotionally watched as the vehicle advanced, one thought flashing through his mind like heat lightning through a calm evening sky. *If I don't move I might get to spend some time in a nice warm hospital.*

At the last possible second, he rolled from the vehicle's path, its tires missing his legs by mere inches. When he regained his composure and stopped swearing at himself for being such a chickenshit, he stared at the tire print that now crossed his coattail, sighed, and remarked in a voice filled with relief, "You couldn't do it! Just couldn't do it, could ya? Thank you, God, I'm not totally screwed up!"

He pictured himself trying to walk, minus his feet, which made him snicker. Then he stated jokingly, "Things are hard enough without that. Would save hunting for shoes though. I never seem to find the right size or a matching pair. Thanks again, God! I have grown quite attached to my feet."

He struggled upright, straightened his clothing as best he could, and spoke with a crispness in his voice that had not been there in years. "Better get moving. Today's the day. Can't be late! I'll miss you, box. Thanks to you, I guess, I have stayed warmer than most."

For the first time in years, Andy did not bother to fold the carton and hide it. Today if someone stole it, well, so be it. One way or another he would not be returning.

The restaurant's rear door opened, and Peppy the dishwasher stepped out into the alley, waving his usual good morning salute to Andy. Andy thought, *it must be seven o'clock. I'm running late!*

He yelled as he started to move away, "Hey there, Peppy. How's it hanging?"

Andy had always liked Peppy, even before he had helped Andy obtain food to eat. Peppy had never badmouthed him or tried to chase him away. Peppy grabbed his crotch and laughed. He thought of himself as a Don Juan and sexual conquest was all he ever had on his mind. His response to Andy was his usual. "Yo, Andy, want to wash some pots for breakfast? Wait till I tell you about the broad I picked up last night."

"No time today, Peppy my man. I'm late," Andy hollered then hurriedly asked, "You know who won the presidential election last night?"

Peppy answered with an I don't give a shit attitude. "Nope, I don't know, don't care. Don't understand why you care either Andy after the way they have treated you!" Peppy was as Andy used to be, not caring about anything but today.

Andy exclaimed, "You should, Peppy! You're going to be sorry when you're older. See ya later. Oh, wow!"

Peppy asked anxiously, "What's wrong, Andy?"

Andy mumbled, "Nothing, Peppy, just forgot something for a moment. You take care, and don't catch any strange sexual diseases." Andy gulped, took a deep breath, then sighed and shook his head slowly. He said to himself, "If all goes according to plan, there is no later. Damn, don't think about it; just get moving. No matter how it goes, it'll be an improvement!"

With two bad hips he could barely walk, and aided by his canes, he painfully headed for the corner of Sesame and Ninth to meet the others. He could not help but wish for the millionth time that the veteran's hospitals had not been overrun first by Vietnamese refugees, then Iraqi refugees, and then illegal immigrants, forcing all the veterans to have their benefits cut.

The government had promised veterans medical benefits for life, but like all government promises, some foreign country needed the funds more than the Americans. And wonder of wonders, of course, the politicians involved always seemed to get richer about the same time. Then Social Security had been allowed to fold. If he had received the hip replacements he was entitled to, he would still be employed and not homeless and would still be receiving his military retirement. He complained loudly to no one in particular, "I was a soldier for twenty-five years, defending this country, then worked and paid my taxes another ten as a civilian. I paid into SSI my entire life. I think that I deserve to receive at least what I paid in. Damn those politicians! I wonder which government leech is cashing my military retirement checks."

His mind constantly rehashed how he had wound up in this black hole of life as he hobbled along. As he stumbled down the sidewalk, he thought, *while I certainly had help, this was mostly my fault. I ignored the government my entire life. I sat back while it squandered taxpayer dollars buying votes from the portions of society that want everything for nothing. All I did was bitch! I watched the government jobs filled with unqualified lazy leeches who received benefits beyond belief and are unfirable. Politicians became filthy rich, cutting deals with foreign countries that were sent billions of our dollars while we sank into poverty. I guess I'm getting what I deserve! I should have taken my role as a citizen more seriously, but I waited too long. The American taxpayer has been sacrificed for political greed, and without anyone changing this cycle of abuse, this country will fall!*

Andy stated firmly to no one in particular, "Today will be the day things begin to change. Maybe I did ignore what the government was doing, but now I can correct my mistake. SCWNH is giving me a second chance."

SCWNH, or Senior Citizens with No Hope, had scheduled an event in the park at noon with a local congressman. Their plan was simple: put the fear of God into politicians and government leeches. Teddy Roosevelt's famous admonition went "speak softly and carry a big stick; you will go far."

Someone in SCWNH had figured out what their membership's big stick was—desperation. Despair is a powerful weapon, especially if coupled with patriotism and anger. Desperate people will willingly perform desperate acts. Andy had listened closely to their plan, pointed out the obvious flaws in the operation, and then immediately became the team leader. He and nine other volunteers were going to spearhead a grassroots movement that would hopefully start the country back in the right direction. Not only would his conscience be salved and his immediate situation improved, but if all went well, he would also go down in history as one of the instigators of great change in this country.

As he approached the designated meeting place he counted. Six, seven, eight, nine, and he made ten. Everyone had shown up.

That was a good sign. No last-minute changes of mind—absolute commitment. They were off to a great start. No one spoke as they headed for the park; everyone knew their role. Andy had made certain of that. They had to be the first in the gates to get upfront because the plan wouldn't work if they could not gain access to the congressman.

The ten were the first to arrive but were forced to wait while the cops set up a portable metal detector to check for weapons. These days a lot of people were extremely upset with their government representatives. Gun makers had followed the tobacco giants into forced oblivion after politicians started having short meetings with bullets from their constituents. All guns had been banned, but handguns were still available.

After all, any competent machine shop could produce them, for the right price.

The ten passed inspection and since all of them walked with canes or crutches, they were allowed to sit down immediately in the front row and were slated to ask the congressman questions. They were each given the question to be asked, written in large print in case of poor eyesight. The ten positioned themselves and waited. All the major television networks were running live feeds. News was scarce. By the time the congressman arrived, the park was full.

The news people outnumbered the participants and pushed them out of the way to get better angles, but that was to be expected. The aged and homeless were not at the top of any popularity poll.

The politician made a lengthy speech about how he cared for the elderly and the homeless, and his absolute concern over the demise of SSI. The meeting then opened for questions from the audience.

Quiet rippled across the spectators as the front row lined up to introduce themselves and pose their queries. The first, a woman, spoke. "My name is Martha Gerard. I'm homeless and terminally ill. My question is, why did you vote to send billions to North Korea and not use that money to help shore up SSI?"

The congressman's aides whispered amongst themselves. This was not a scheduled question. The congressman took a deep breath and answered in a terse voice, "Well now, Martha, that's a complicated issue. I have to vote my conscience and we need to keep North Korea peaceful. Besides, their people were starving! Next question, please."

The congressman looked as if someone had just fed him a sour lemon and he shot his top aide a nasty stare. The aide was an aspiring politician herself and she understood quite well. Number two talked loudly and very quickly. "My name is

Samuel Perkins and I'm homeless. Were you in SSI or did you, like most politicians, opt for a private retirement federally funded plan?"

With a face suddenly tinged in red, the congressman answered smoothly. "Sam, my personal finances are a private matter, but I will say that if I was not enrolled in SSI, the law gave me that choice and I exercised my legal rights. Next question!" The congressman's look became even sourer and his aide looked as if she was about to kill someone.

Then the third questioner asked, "I'm Andy Donovan, a decorated veteran and homeless. Didn't Congress initiate the law that allowed politicians and federal employees to opt out of SSI? So, in essence, did you not as a congressman take care of yourself at everyone else's expense?"

The congressman's voice could have cut glass as he bit off his response. "That's two questions, and the answers are a matter of public record. Next!"

The crowd emitted a loud groan. The

congressman's aide hurried to the microphone and declared, "Now listen up folks, the congressman was nice enough to take time from his busy schedule and come here to listen to you and answer your questions. You should be thankful!"

A voice from the crowd rang clear as a bell. "He's here because the golf course is closed, his mistress can't see him because his wife is in town, and he wanted to get on TV. If you tell me I'm wrong, you're a liar."

Nasty laughter erupted from the crowd, and the aide continued tersely, "One question apiece, and if the crowd can't control itself, our security can, and the congressman will leave. Now, who's next?"

The ten members of SCWNH looked at each other, then nodded in unison. One stepped forward, moving slowly on his crutches. "I'm Howard Avery, homeless like the rest. May I apologize for the inappropriate behavior and shake the congressman's hand?"

Boos, hisses, and catcalls came from the crowd, and the congressman waited until they had subsided before he answered. "Sure, Howie, I'll shake with you. It's about time someone showed a little gratitude for what I do for my constituents." He turned to his aide and, forgetting that his shirt microphone broadcast every word, said in a whisper, "Who do these old assholes think they are? Whoever scheduled this event is fired. Hear me? Fired! I'm going to shake his filthy hand then get the hell out of here. There's not a legal voter in this park. Not one of these filthy misfits has a residence. How can they vote? Get my limo ready."

The politician's aide tried to warn him that his shirt mike was still broadcasting, but the congressman was so upset that he ignored her. He stepped forward and grabbed Avery's hand, wincing as his fingers were compressed tightly.

Avery spoke, "I'm sorry for a lot, Mr.

Congressman. Mostly for my indifference over what you crooks in the government were doing. I might be a filthy bum now, but I didn't used to be, and I always paid my taxes. And by the way, the whole world heard what you said and can still hear us."

The congressman tried to let go and couldn't, finally, he screamed, "Get this old bum off me!"

Avery pulled the congressman into the crowd. The aide had enough sense to run, and the security detail tried to intervene but wasn't fast enough. Ten people on crutches and canes surrounded the politician and the crowd surged around the ten, keeping the security at bay.

Andy Donavan spoke loudly, "Careful folks, don't break his microphone." The ex-Green Beret then struck the first blow. He slammed his cane into the congressman's temple knocking him to his knees.

Nine people joined Andy in hitting the politician repeatedly as hard as they could, their actions broadcast over national television during prime time. The TV audience was able to view each blow in slow motion, hear every grunt, groan, and impact. The ten made sure that the TV crews had access for their cameras. When the politician ceased all movement, each of the ten delivered one final blow, stating in unison. "This is for God and country."

As Margaret Delaney kicked her last kick, she was shot in the head by a security guard and fell directly on top of the congressman's battered remains. The fact that politicians and their bodyguards were still allowed to own guns for self-protection was not forgotten in the aftermath. At least the bullet saved Margaret from six months of a slow, agonizing death. The crowd surged, and the guard met the same fate as the congressman while all America bore witness in digital quality and surround sound.

A spokesman for the SCWNH gave an instant statement to the press. "These ten are martyrs for our cause. We feel that if we had not collectively ignored the government's abuse of power the country would not be in its present situation. We, eighteen million strong and growing, will do what we feel is necessary to bring back a people's government. This is no longer a government by and for the people, but rather a government paid for by the people and abused by politicians and government employees. Fear us, politicians, for you are given notice. Your days are numbered. And for all the leeches that have been sucking the blood from the American taxpayer by posing as government workers, beware! The next time you are about to abuse someone in your arrogance, think of today. We helped make this problem by our indifference, and now in our despair, we have nothing to lose. These ten will have a better life in jail than they could on the street and remember, they are but the minuscule tip of the iceberg. And for those politicians, their lackeys, and government leeches of all races, religions, and ethnic backgrounds who think that they will be able to foil us with technology and by keeping themselves from close proximity with those in the SCWNH, I have news for you! Many of the very persons who designed the metal detectors and sophisticated alarm systems, etc. are part of the citizens that you have exploited and now wish to ignore into oblivion. They were intelligent enough to design them, we're certain they are desperate enough to figure out how to circumvent them.

"Also remember that you have to sleep, use a restroom, go to church to salve your guilty conscience, and eat. The only way to keep us from your door is to leave the country. We don't care if you hide in one of the country's most secure bunkers; we have access to the people who designed and built it. As of today, you have a target on your forehead. The only way to remove that threat is to start doing your jobs and taking care of the business for the people of this country instead of yourselves and foreign interests.

"For those government workers who are doing your jobs, you are safe, but keep in mind that your fifty-two holidays a year, ninety days personal time per year, ninety-three days sick time per year, and anytime it snows, or your boss or you had a good time with your significant other, you can have off, still being paid five and a half times more than normal and having special health care and retirement one hundred percent funded, must stop. You must become accountable. Yes, some of you must be fired! You can help us stop it, or we will stop it permanently!"

All television sets went to commercial after this statement, leaving the after images of the congressman's battered remains imprinted on every viewer's brain. The government tried to play down the event for days afterward, but other acts of violent retribution made that almost impossible. Shootings, stabbings, poisonings, and beatings became almost a daily occurrence.

As Andy lay down on his first mattress in over two years, after seeing his first doctor in five, after his first shower and first real meal in a year, after his first painkiller in three, looking up at the first roof in two, he smoothed his first clean clothes in what seemed like forever and burst into the first long belly laugh in ten years.

"What's so funny Andy?" This guard was overly friendly, not like the ones on the day shift; he had caught the news on TV just before coming to work. Several federal border guards had been caught in a bar while supposedly on duty and had been hung from a nearby porch roof.

Between guffaws, Andy answered. "I remember all my life I didn't want to go to jail. Bad food, sadistic guards, Bubba waiting for you to bend over to pick up the soap, all the stuff to make a person walk the straight and narrow. Now here I am in jail, so happy I don't know what to do. Ironic huh?"

Andy started laughing too hard to talk. From

eight other cells down the aisle, peals of laughter joined in. The guard stood and shuffled his feet then pulled his shirtsleeve around to where he could read the patch. Federal Department of Corrections.

He muttered to himself for a long while after staring at the government insignia. Snores had replaced the prisoners' laughter. Calm, peaceful, contented snores. Suddenly, the guard spoke to himself quietly. "Might as well wear a bull's-eye. I do my job. I work my three days a week. I do have it better than everyone else and I know it's not really right, but...hmm...maybe I could cut some of my benefits and they could be given to the old and needy.... Nah! The boss would just think I was crazy and fire me."

He continued mumbling to himself as the tedious hours of his shift dragged by slowly. Then just before he was due to be relieved, his face lit with the glow of an epiphany. He thought, *wouldn't want to say this out loud. I'm going to contact the SCWNH and see what I can do to help, and I bet I'll not be alone!*

Teddy

P am Sterling made a huge mistake during her senior year. She got drunk at a teen party and went home with a guy she didn't know. The next morning, after waking up in the emergency room, she discovered that the guy had gifted her a problem, and sometime later she discovered the second. One was a hospital bill for her assault that he denied committing, and two, a pregnancy from the sexual acts that he said never happened.

A DNA test proved that he definitely had sex with her, so he apologized and stated that he had been too drunk to remember but was absolutely certain it had been consensual sex. After all, he would never harm any woman, especially one that he had fallen in love with at first sight. Pam had been too inebriated to remember anything, and after he wined and dined her several times, she had the criminal charges dropped. Two months later, the day after she graduated high school and turned eighteen, he asked her to move in with him so that he could support her and their baby.

Pam's parents tried to talk sense to her, but when all their arguments fell on deaf ears, they disowned her. One month later she was back in the hospital with several broken ribs, a smashed nose, and a few missing teeth. While the doctors were examining her they discovered that she was actually having twins, a girl and a boy. Her so-called boyfriend, Sam Alito, told the police that Pam had been mugged outside the local bar while he was in the restroom. The police noted that Sam's right hand had a large white bandage wrapped around its knuckles.

When questioned about how his hand had become injured, Sam swore that he had been in a bar fight. Upon investigating, the police could find no one else in the bar that had witnessed any fight, let alone one involving Sam. Sam then told the police that it wasn't actually in the bar but in the restroom, and only he and his attacker were present. Pam swore she couldn't remember anything until she had woken up in the hospital.

Sam was a known woman abuser, but the police had not been able to get any of his victims to testify against him. Pam's lack of memories forced the police to allow Sam to skate on yet another assault charge.

The close call with the cops scared Sam enough that he cut back on his drinking and treated Pam decently for several months. Then one evening, a neighbor called the police, reporting screams coming from the Alito's residence. When the police arrived, they found Pam unconscious, lying on the floor with a naked Sam kicking her repeatedly in the stomach. They arrested Sam for aggravated assault and rushed Pam to the hospital.

The doctors immediately informed both Pam and the Police that the babies were OK and that the only thing that had kept the babies alive was the fact that Sam had been barefoot; a rigid shoe would have probably killed both babies. Pam spent the remaining time of her pregnancy in a hospital bed with her doctors reassuring her that both of her babies were alive and well.

Sam, while still in the police car on the way to jail, informed the police that he didn't really want to hurt Pam, he had just been trying to kill the babies because he didn't want to have to support them. The charges were immediately changed from assault to two counts of attempted murder. Sam's attorney managed to get the charges dropped by saying the police questioned his client while he was still drunk and unable to defend himself. Sam's sobriety test backed his claim and the judge not only dropped the charges but ordered the police to stay away from Sam. Sam turned and gave the cops sitting in the courtroom the finger and when the prosecutor complained, the judge stated that the incompetent cops were getting what they deserved.

After several weeks, Sam started to visit Pam in the hospital daily, bringing her flowers and candy each time. He apologized profusely to her and treated her like a queen. The police tried to bar him from visits, but the same judge ordered them to leave Sam alone. Then Pam made her third major mistake. She allowed the abusive hypocrite to convince her that he had quit drinking and had turned over a new leaf. He kept telling her that all he wanted out of life was her and their two kids. They were married in the hospital by Sam's friendly personal judge.

Pam delivered no boy, just one baby girl! The doctors were astonished. There was absolutely no medical answer for what had happened to the second baby. Pam's ultrasounds, taken the day before delivery, definitely showed two infants, although the boy's image was a little vague and misty. Pam and the baby girl went home with Sam the following week against the advice of the police.

For seven years, Sam didn't come home when he drank; he spent the night somewhere else. Of course, other women were assaulted and some claimed that Sam was responsible. The police kept picking Sam up for questioning and asking Pam repeatedly if Sam had confided in her about any of the assaults. Sam's friendly judge dismissed Sam's charges repeatedly and finally found two cops guilty of harassing Sam. Both were fired immediately!

Pam lived in constant fear. She knew that sooner or later Sam was going to be unable to find someone to beat up and he would come home drunk and in a very bad mood. She and her daughter, Jo, would pay the price. It was just a matter of time! Pam tried to leave Sam but she had nowhere to go. Her parents slammed their door in her face and refused to answer her calls. She made emergency plans. Anytime Sam wasn't home by six, she and Jo stayed the night in the garden shed in the backyard with the door locked.

During this time, Jo kept telling her mom about her buddy. A little boy Jo's age who could change size and even become invisible. His name was Teddy; Jo had named him after her favorite bear. Pam told Jo that Teddy wasn't real, but Jo's stories of Teddy's exploits became more and more dramatic and explicit. Most of Jo's tales of Teddy's triumphs were about Teddy conquering large vicious dogs and cats that had bothered Jo.

The neighborhood became petless. The bodies of the pets were always found shriveled and emaciated, covered with a bluish tinge. No one, including the police, had a clue about what had killed them. Most people came to the conclusion that someone living close by had poisoned them. Pam had her own ideas!

Then one night, Sam arrived home staggering drunk. He searched the house, smashing anything that he tripped over or fell into or onto. He yelled and screamed for Jo and Pam to stop hiding and come out where he could see them. He promised not to harm them then promptly smashed the nearest object. After an hour or so, he finally arrived at the garden shed door. The police had been called by the neighbors, but, remembering the two fired cops, they were in no hurry to intervene.

Sam asked Pam, in a voice that was so slurred that Pam could hardly understand him, to let him into the shed. When she screamed for him to go away, he busted his empty Tequila bottle on the door and kicked it until the lock broke. Pam was standing just inside and had Jo hiding behind some fertilizer bags to her rear. Pam started crying and begged Sam to leave them alone. He grabbed her by the neck with both hands and started to shake and choke her at the same time. Jo came out of hiding and tried to help her mom by kicking Sam in the ankle. Sam let go of Pam's throat, punched her in the forehead, and grabbed Jo. Pam fell to the ground, knocked unconscious. Jo wailed at the top of her lungs until Sam shook her so hard she fainted.

Then the weird stuff started that, thank God, no one but Sam got to see or experience. A mist developed around Jo, rapidly becoming denser and larger. It floated from her and enveloped Sam. Sam dropped Jo and clawed at the solidifying mist. It suddenly disappeared and Sam became rigid, standing frozen for several minutes. He vomited almost pure Tequila, then turned and left the garden shed, pulling out his pocket knife as he walked in a very stilted, stiff-legged manner, like a puppet on a string.

Sirens announced the arrival of the police, and Sam headed in their direction. As he came into their view he stopped, unbuckled his pants, and dropped them down around his ankles. He then dropped his shorts and stood naked in full view of the cops and his neighbors. He danced a little jig and then punched himself in the nose until blood ran down his chin. When the police yelled for him to freeze, Sam laughed at them and gave them the finger with his left hand.

Moving deliberately and slowly, he opened the blade on his knife and stood staring at the night sky for several seconds, then, in slow motion, never uttering one word or showing any signs of pain or hesitation, he sawed off both his penis and testicles with its short dull blade. When he finished cutting, he stuck the knife up to its hilt into his chest and stood frozen, bleeding profusely, rivers of blood cascading down the insides of his legs and chest. The cops watched in amazement during the very short time required for him to bleed to death.

The police never reported the fact that after his death Sam looked like a shrunken, wrinkled doll with a blue tinge covering his entire body. One cop remarked that Sam's remains reminded him of all the dead pets that had been found in this neighborhood. Maybe Sam was the poisoner and had imbibed his own poison. Everyone stared at the bloody spectacle of Sam's private parts but didn't notice the wisp of mist that left Sam and entered Jo.

Pam and Jo were rushed to the hospital and declared OK. The judge held a hearing to ascertain whether the police had done their jobs or had allowed Sam to die in an act of revenge. The judge forced Jo to testify and had her crying violently within minutes during his questioning. Pam rushed to her daughter's side and called the judge several nasty names in a very loud voice. After doing a little cussing himself, the judge found Pam in contempt of court and fined her one thousand dollars or thirty days in jail.

The police were vindicated by Pam and Jo's testimony, backed by the cameras that the cops were forced to wear. After the decision was heard, one police captain lost his temper and yelled at the judge that this entire happening was the judge's fault. The judge lost his temper and ordered everyone out of his courtroom in a highly agitated tone and using profanity. Before leaving, all persons present in that courtroom voiced their agreement with the captain. The police officers and other spectators contributed enough money to pay Pam's fine.

Several weeks later, the judge was removed from the bench after hitting a witness on the forehead with his gavel for telling the judge to kiss his ass. Drug testing was mandatory for the police investigation and the drug test showed that the judge had been smoking weed. The police also uncovered the fact that Sam was actually the judge's cousin. Disbarment procedures commenced immediately.

Several days later, the judge was found lying in his living room with his throat cut, the knife still clenched in his right hand. The coroner found that it was suicide, but no one could figure out why the body was so shriveled and covered with a blue tinge. The judge looked as if he hadn't eaten in weeks.

No one noticed or thought that the fact that the judge had visited Pam and Jo in the hospital might be pertinent. The nurses, however, did report the Judge's extremely loud voice and swearing coming from Pam's room. When Jo and Pam were reunited, the first thing Jo told her mom was that Teddy had gotten even for her. Pam just giggled and hugged Jo harder, after all, every kid had their fantasy hero and friend! Hers had been Wonder Woman.

Throughout her childhood, Jo always said that if anyone bothered her Teddy would get them. Pam started believing in Teddy after many weird happenings occurred. The demise of local pets was at the top of her list. She herself had almost envisioned Teddy on several occasions while disciplining Jo for bad behavior. The mist, or as Jo called it, Teddy, would start forming, then slowly disappear as if Teddy had thought things over and decided to let Mom alone. Then Pam made another huge mistake. She talked to a welfare shrink about Teddy and mentioned the strange occurrences that had happened during the past few years. She went into explicit details about Teddy and Jo's relationship, pointing out Teddy's protective actions.

The shrink had a few meetings with Jo and then acted like Santa had just visited. She informed Pam that she was going to commit Jo to a government hospital for further testing. Pam said she wouldn't allow it to happen and immediately tried to leave with Jo. Suddenly, three men in cheap black suits entered the room and physically restrained her. Jo kicked one of them in the knee. The shrink grabbed Jo. The mist formed and Teddy appeared. He enveloped one of Pam's attackers, who promptly pulled his pistol and shot the other two and the shrink all in the head. The attacker was still standing over his victims, gun in hand, when the local police arrived and shot him numerous times. He died immediately, his body's blue tinge readily visible.

One of the arriving cops, while helping Pam and Jo leave the room, remarked that the shooter looked malnourished and was probably using drugs due to his appearance and blue tinge. No one noticed but Jo as Teddy absorbed himself back into her. Pam and Jo were kept on scene until another black suit-clad overbearing dipshit showed up. He walked around issuing orders like he thought he owned everybody and everything. He finally slithered over and informed Pam that she and her daughter had to go with him for further questioning.

Before Pam could say anything, the suit-clad asshole grabbed Jo by the arm and started dragging her towards the door. Jo squealed in surprise and pain as he twisted her arm. This time Teddy literally popped out of Jo and immersed the suit immediately. The suit's eyes bugged out, he started gasping for breath, and his neck turned bright red as his own hands squeezed it violently. His hands twisted to the right and then back to the left rapidly. A loud pop announced that the suit's neck had broken. The body hit the floor so hard that it bounced.

The cops who were still in the room watched in amazement as Teddy reappeared and reunited with his sister. After several seconds passed, Teddy visited the cops who were still staring at Jo, one after the other. When he had visited all the cops present, he wafted his way back to Jo and disappeared again. The cops shook their heads in bewilderment and left the room. Later when they were questioned, the cops all stated that the suit-clad dipshit had committed suicide by strangling himself. Pam's statement was a mirror image of the cops. Talk about an unbelievable scenario.

The person doing the interrogation was decent enough, and lucky enough, to not bother Jo. Again, thank goodness, no one seemed to notice the underweight bodies or the tell-tale blue tinge.

Pam had seen enough to know that the government had taken a great interest in Teddy. She thought about how hilarious it was for the government to know about Teddy and what he was capable of doing and still show up and scare Jo. Guess the dumbasses had received what they deserved. She packed up and she, Jo, and Teddy hit the road.

For over ten years the threesome traveled the country doing odd jobs and staying nowhere more than several weeks. They were very careful to avoid any actions that would incite Teddy to slip into protection mode. During that time, Teddy became able to exist on his own. Although his shape had a small tendency to shift slightly, almost no one ever noticed. He looked, talked, and dressed like a male version of his twin sister.

Both twins were extremely intelligent and Pam homeschooled them easily. The main difference between the twins was that Jo wouldn't ever think about killing anything, she wouldn't even step on a roach. Teddy, however, was the exact opposite. His first impulse was to kill, and, using the roaches as an example, if he had his way he would not only stomp on it but grind it into mush with his shoe. Then he would track down and kill the entire nest.

Pam tried desperately to no avail to calm Teddy down, but no one bothered Jo, or Teddy came unglued. After watching Teddy consume the life forces of animals for a year or so, Pam was finally able to get him to absorb only what he needed and quit before the animals died. The fact that he was leaving a trail of blue-tinged carcasses that the government could easily follow finally convinced Teddy to follow Pam's suggestion. He ultimately told Pam that eating less from more victims made them taste much better than if he ate them until they died.

The nomad life became normal living for the trio. Then Pam had a heart attack and died in her sleep. Jo and Teddy had just turned eighteen and were devastated. They sat in a small sandwich shop. While Jo ate lunch, they were discussing their future plans when a black guy with a gun decided to rob the place. He made the mistake of pointing the gun at Jo and wound up shooting himself in the head, his blue tinge almost unnoticeable due to his black skin. Jo and Teddy left immediately but were captured on the store's security cameras. The video clearly showed Teddy dissolving and entering the robber's head, then, after the suicide, Teddy very clearly traveled back to his own form. The local police immediately put out an arrest on-sight alert. Jo and Teddy's vehicle was stopped the next day as they attempted to leave town.

The police approached their car with guns drawn. Teddy for some reason decided to mist himself into Jo, probably thinking to keep her safer. All the cops witnessed was Jo jerking about and screaming for Teddy to stop moving. No one ever figured out which cop shot first, or why, but Jo was shot nineteen times. All that was discovered in the car was Jo's unarmed body and Teddy's empty clothing. The cops were all charged with excessive force and terminated. Teddy was never seen again.

Within six months, four of the ex-cops involved in Jo's death had committed suicide, none were tinged blue, although they were all slightly thinner. The FBI investigated and stated that the weight loss was probably due to depression-related problems because of their being fired.

Guess Teddy had actually learned to curb his appetite!

Eat less for a better taste!

Cain and Rodney

Cain squatted just inside the rear door of his older brother Rodney's house, his back against the wall, his head bowed, staring at the design in the new linoleum that had been recently installed on the kitchen floor. He had to admit that the new floor covering should be much easier to clean than the former well-worn oak planks and much more sanitary. But still, it wasn't that big of a deal.

The entire family had been summoned by Rodney to celebrate this momentous occasion and all were present from grandparents to grandkids. Scattered around the house, they talked, fought, and played, never once including Cain. Totally ignored as always, he imagined that the lines on the floor were roads and that he was cruising them on his bike, a 113 cubic inch rigid Harley clone. Lost in this fantasy, he leaned into a hard turn so far that the kickstand scraped asphalt, producing a burst of multi-colored sparks. He banged the transmission into third and hammered the throttle, the bike squirming as if it were alive and able to enjoy flexing its awesome power. He popped it back into fourth gear, exited the curve, straightened up, and then twisted the throttle to the stops. The front wheel rose a foot into the air and he sat absolutely frozen while he eased off the gas until it touched the road again. The wind tore at him, but he sat on his bike, expertly performing a balancing act. His bike had no speedometer, but he imagined his speed at about one-thirty, or maybe even one-forty.

Adrenaline rushes, even fantasy ones, were always thrilling, but something was missing. His mind shifted to Manda. Suddenly he was with her, explaining to the busty, skimpily-clad female that riding his bike was like sitting on a bowl of Jello on the back of a speeding semi traveling down an extremely bumpy road. God what an experience, the best feeling ever! Riding the edge, heart pumping, adrenaline flowing, and scared shitless—the absolute essence of being alive.

Manda stood on her tiptoes to whisper in his ear in that voice that sent chills down his back and made it difficult to talk or walk. "You think that feels better than these?"

She stepped back and slowly removed her bikini top. As he reached for her, he stated emphatically, "Aw shit! It used to be, but I could be persuaded!" Cain found himself kissing linoleum instead of Manda, with all present staring at him. He quickly scrambled to his feet and muttered, "Now I know how E.F. Hutton felt, 'cause I talked and everyone listened."

No one laughed or cracked as much as a small

smile.

"What are you doing, Cain?" Rodney's voice had all the unpleasant attributes of a Honda crotch rocket's screeching exhaust.

Cain sighed deeply, wishing for the umpteenth time he had not come. Then he muttered, "Shit! I'm not doing anything; I just slipped."

Rodney quipped, "Well, before you fell over, you looked like one of the dogs when they dream and woof in their sleep! And you know better than to swear in front of my damn kids, asshole."

Everyone laughed loudly at Rodney's crude joke then quit at exactly the same time, as if somehow Rodney had turned them on and off. Now Rodney seemed to have switched them to stare mode because Cain was sure getting the dirty looks. He spoke quietly, "Yeah, thanks, Rodney, I like you too. I hadn't realized that I swore. I fucken apologize."

Cain stretched, his lanky six-foot-two-inch frame towering over everyone present. He had always been the odd one in this family. Tall with long bright red hair. He stood out like a puke-green Suzuki at the Harley dealer. All his family members were short and chunky with thin sandy brown hair. They had always seemed to resent Cain with a passion bordering on hatred, especially Rodney. Ugly always seems to hate handsome for some reason.

Cain picked up his leather jacket and stuffed his left arm into the sleeve. Rodney's next words made him pause. "Got one for ya! A really good one!"

Cain slowly finished putting on his jacket, shook his head no, and spoke in a quiet disgusted tone, "Wondered why you invited me. Aren't we getting a little old for this shit?"

Rodney continued, "This is a good one, Baby Brother. I promise. Besides, not only do you get to show how manly you are, there's also money to be made."

Cain spoke slowly, thinking as he talked. "You

know, Rodney, ever since we were kids, you've been trying to scare, or kill me, and most of the time I'm never quite sure which. I've won every one of your asinine bets. I used to think they were fun, now they're just like you, stupid. I'm leaving!"

Rodney spouted, "What's the matter Cain, chicken? C l u c k, c l u c k."

Cain's voice sounded disgusted as he responded, "No Rodney, I just have better things to do."

Cain closed Rodney's door behind him, mentally patting himself on the back and thanking Manda's vision for its help. He had been able to walk away from Rodney's bullshit for the first time in his life. He ambled down the sidewalk to his bike, his only thoughts, an enjoyable ride to Manda's house, then several hours of pure uninhibited sex, followed by steak and eggs.

But as he sat on his bike in the still evening air, pulling on his gloves, peals of laughter came from the house. His entire family was inside laughing at him. He kicked his bike's big motor over and it started immediately. He sat while it warmed up, listening to their laughter, still clear over his exhaust's mellow thump thump. Pride rose to drown his common sense and cause his desire for Manda to fade. He blipped the throttle several times, knowing that although the deep rumble created was music to him, his family hated that sound with a passion. He slipped the transmission into first, hesitated for several seconds, sighed a long deep regretful sigh, and then shifted it back into neutral. He shut his bike off, dropped the kickstand, and headed back into the house. No one was going to laugh at him, especially not Rodney; besides, the roads to Manda's were all flat and straight!

Rodney's response as he entered the kitchen infuriated Cain and caused everyone else to laugh uproariously. Rodney quipped between chuckles, "Told ya superboy'd be back."

Cain spoke tersely, mad at himself for allowing

Rodney to push his buttons once again and for being so easily manipulated. "What game we playing this time, Rodney?"

Rodney's voice sounded like a fake preacher thanking an idiot for giving him a large amount of money. "Our last game, Baby Brother. The last one. I promise you."

"Well talk, Rodney. I want to get this over with."

Cain was so tired. He had been putting up with Rodney's BS his entire life. He just wanted this all to end. He couldn't help but wish that he had the balls to just knock Rodney's teeth out and then leave forever.

Rodney spoke while sporting a smile so large that all his teeth were visible like a Piranha fish getting ready to bite. "OK, Cain! It's easy. If you're not too scared, you'll go into a deserted house and bring back a little box. It's as simple as that."

Cain erupted, "Rodney, you asshole! I'm not a

burglar. Go break into the house yourself. What do you think I am, an idiot?"

Rodney responded quickly, "No Cain, listen! This's legal. The owner himself will even pay you to do it!"

Strangely, Rodney sounded believable and Cain found himself saying, "Rodney, with you, nothing's simple. You're always trying to get me maimed or killed. What's the catch? Tell me quick or I'm leaving!" Cain moved towards the front door, as he talked.

Rodney erupted, "Wait! Stop! Don't leave. No catch, at least no catch that would worry a guy as macho as you! Art Wilson, Sam Wilson's brother, you know Sam. He owns the Titty Twister bar in Albion. They've lived there for twenty years. Anyway, one day out of the blue, Art visits Sam and says he's dying." Rodney spoke quickly and was hard to understand.

Cain cut him off with a sharp retort. "No! Rodney, I don't know him, but I've heard you speak of King Sam."

"King? What are you talking about, Cain?"

Rodney sounded miffed, and Cain laughed as he declared, "King of you rednecks. Aw forget it, Rodney. Get on with your bullshit."

Rodney continued at a slightly slower pace, "OK, like I was saying before you so rudely interrupted, Art tells Sam that he's dying and that he would leave the property title for the family farm in a box in the house and that following his death, if Sam would retrieve it, he could sell the farm. After Art's funeral, Sam hired men to get the deed, and they all disappeared while trying. Since your balls are so big, Cain, I double dog dare you to go into that house and retrieve the box." Rodney was forced to take a deep breath after such a long and passionate speech.

Cain again moved to depart as he declared, "Rodney your story's so lame. I'm going now and I won't be back. Been thinking about joining the army."

Rodney sounded desperate as he spoke. "I double dog dare ya again, Cain, and if you don't, everyone in the county will call you a chicken and know it's true."

Cain kept moving towards the door. Rodney started to cluck, and the entire family joined in. Cain turned and, with great anger, spoke his piece. "I'll do it! I'll do it right now! I know how stupid I'm being, but when this is over, and I make Rodney look a fool for the umpteenth time, I'm history. The rest of you can call me chicken anytime you want, but you'll have to do it long distance. Let's go, Rodney. Let's get this bull shit over with!"

The sun was setting as they arrived at a large Midwest-style farmhouse, Cain berating himself the entire way there. "If I had any brains I'd have at least waited until tomorrow. But oh no! Let Rodney call me chicken and here I am, about to play another of his games and at night. I'm sure stupid!"

Evidently, Rodney's entire pack of buds was here because about a dozen vehicles, including the sheriff's, were parked randomly about the yard. Cain cracked the throttle on his bike, allowing the bark of the drag pipes to announce his arrival. As he ambled up the sidewalk, those present parted like a group of Christians before an attacking coliseum lion. Cain mumbled as he walked, "Wonder why bikers always make rednecks nervous?" Then he stated loudly, "Don't have any corn in my pockets today boys, your women are safe, at least for now!"

He ignored their muttering, they weren't drunk enough yet to be dangerous. As he topped the front steps, the sheriff waddled forward and spoke. "Hold it, cycle bum! You sure you want to do this? We still haven't found the others. We searched this house after each disappearance and never found a trace. Art Wilson was an oddball, hard to tell how he booby-trapped his house. He hated his brother, Sam, with a passion and always thought he was smarter than anyone else. I'm not sure, but I think he was some kind of scientist!"

Cain spoke politely, his curiosity aroused by his common sense, "Thanks for your concern, Sheriff, seems like brothers who hate each other are easy to find around here. If you don't believe me, just ask Rodney. Hey, I was wondering, why didn't you get the box while you were in there and make yourself some bucks?"

The sheriff sounded a little perturbed as he answered. "It was gone, motor mouth, that's why. Quit while you still can."

"Yeah, chicken out, Cain. C l u c k, c l u c k, c l u c k." Good old Rodney, he always knew what buttons to push.

Cain asked quickly before the entire motley bunch started to cluck, "Where's the guy with the bucks?"

A short fat guy stepped forward and answered. "I have a check for ten thousand dollars, all I have to do is fill in your name."

"Ten grand, whoa! Who do I have to kill, Chubby?" Cain was starting to enjoy this and his voice reflected it. Besides he could sure use the money.

Chubby responded in a very arrogant tone, "No one, you idiot! My name is Sam Wilson. Mr. Wilson to you!" Sam not only looked like a fat prick but he even sounded like one!

Cain responded, "Well, mister, you must be the only person in this county shorter and uglier than my brother, Rodney."

Wilson ignored Cain's remark and commanded, "Look through this window."

He aimed a flashlight beam through the glass and spotlighted a table, then continued. "You have to go down the hall from the front door. The first door to your left is the living room. You see that small brown box on the table? Bring it back to me, and the money is yours."

Cain pondered the view then ambled to the front door. He placed his right hand on the doorknob and then suddenly spun on his heel and spoke in a hard flat voice that demanded notice. "Let's get this straight, Mr. Wilson. You're going to pay me ten grand for getting that little box? Others have tried and sort of lost their way, right?"

Instead of Wilson, the sheriff answered. "Five have tried and we've never found any of them. We tried to watch the last one through the window, but the front door won't open until everyone's off the porch. Once you're out in the yard you can't see a damn thing. All five were armed; the last one had a sawed-off twelve-gauge shotgun and we never heard a sound."

Cain unholstered his .45 automatic and chambered a round.

"That's illegal!" spouted the sheriff.

Cain's voice thundered, "Arrest me when I get back, Sheriff. I'll have more than enough money to pay my fine. Just understand this! Anyone who jumps out and yells 'boo' just made a fatal mistake." Cain hesitated, allowing anyone time to speak, then continued. "I'm telling ya again, if someone bothers me while I'm in there, I'll dust his ass. Understand?"

Cain waited long enough to allow the sheriff to answer or stop him, and for all present to remove themselves from the porch. Then he opened the door. He exclaimed over his shoulder loudly before entering, "Be right back. Don't lose my check, mister chubby. This is going to be the easiest money I ever made."

The door closed behind him and Cain distinctly heard the lock snap shut. His heart was pounding. His mouth was dry and sweat streamed from his armpits. His every sense screamed, run! What a wonderful combination, alive to the max, every atom of his body focused. He murmured, "I just might miss playing with Rodney."

The hall was dark; the only light available the moonlight that filtered through the living room door's window and cast shadows that seemed to move with a life of their own. He continued to talk very quietly to himself as he stood just inside the front door. "How could someone disappear in so short a distance? Has to be one of Rodney's tricks. A hole in the floor maybe? What's he up to?"

Cain hefted his .45, its weight comforting. The safety was off, the hammer was back, and the slack was out of the trigger. He raised his voice. "Anyone who fucks around is about to own a 145-grain, hand-loaded hollow point. I'm ready to rock and roll. Are you?"

He took two rapid steps forward, the floorboards squeaking loudly, and then froze. He started counting silently. He tried to concentrate, but the house's creaks and groans, plus its weird shadows, supplied his imagination with things slithering up the hall in his direction. He closed his eyes and pictured Rodney clucking, and everything returned to its proper perspective. He murmured, "It sure plays hell with your timing when the guy you're trying to ambush is late and unpredictable, huh?" His voice was barely audible, even to his ears.

When he reached one hundred, he took off down the hall like a redneck chasing a beer truck. When he turned left into the living room, he had to ricochet himself off the doorpost to complete the turn. He snatched the box as he went past the table and had only enough time to get his arm up over his face before he crashed through the front window. He landed on the porch in a shower of curtains and broken glass and snapped to the rear in case he was being pursued. When no one appeared in the window, he turned to the approaching mob and demanded, "Payday! What a joke! Where's my money, Short Shit?"

Wilson ran to Cain and screamed, "Give it to me! I can't believe you did it! Finally, I can sell this place."

Cain's response was cryptic. "Check first, asshole!"

A powerful voice from the house interrupted, it was not loud enough for those in the yard to hear, but Cain and Wilson heard it plainly. "You did not play the game, Sam Wilson. You do not deserve the deed. You were required to participate, not send others."

Cain stared into the shadows beyond the smashed window over his gun barrel. At first, he saw nothing but then discerned a faint outline in the center of the room. It moved closer and into the moonlight enough for him to see a strange specter. It stood about five-foot-eight. A slender figure dressed in boots and in Levis held up by a belt with a large silver buckle. He was bare from the waist up and carried a sword that reflected the moonlight. Belts crossed his muscular chest and another sword handle jutted above his left shoulder. Cain could not see facial features, but the voice imparted strength and integrity.

Wilson yelled at the top of his lungs, "Give me that box! Give it to me or the boys will take it off your dead body!"

Cain turned his head just enough to see the

entire motley crew drop their beer cans and head for the porch steps. He responded, "Hey, Sheriff, you going to allow these ass poppers to attack me? Don't I have the right to defend myself?"

Rodney's voice answered, "Tough luck, Cain. The sheriff was called away while you were inside. What's the matter, Baby Brother, scared? C l u c k, c l u c k."

Cain's voice made him sound amused. "I have a Colt .45 loaded with a full clip of hollow points. What're you going to do, Rodney? Throw empty beer cans? You never were very intelligent."

Rodney was enjoying himself and his voice mirrored his mood. "Oh, I'm smart enough to know that when you shoot someone I win, and you're going to spend the rest of your life in jail. And, I'm smart enough that I'm going to own this property for ten grand less than Sam wants. Give him the box and get the hell out of here!"

Cain responded nonchalantly, "Well, Rodney, I think you're right, I shouldn't shoot. But do your buds know how good I am at cutting things?"

The .45 disappeared and a four-and-one-half-inch blade snapped open in Cain's right hand. Cain's voice was filled with excitement. "Are you dorks drunk enough to get yourself cut up for ugly and uglier? I can slice and dice a lot before someone dies. And being cut hurts, actually more like a burn though, a real bad burn. You want this box, boys? Come and take it, I dare ya!"

He set his feet and flipped the knife around a few times so the moonlight would glint off the blade. The rednecks stopped their advance then started to move forward slowly as the good old boys in the rear pushed their buds onward, planning to use them for shields.

Wilson demanded, "Last chance, trash. Give me the deed and we'll leave you alone."

Cain glanced at the box then asked, "What about my check?"

Wilson responded, "Your choice, my box or

your ass, but either way, absolutely no money!"

Cain held the box out and Wilson started to reach for his prize then quipped, "Now, you're getting smart, shithead."

As Wilson's fingertips brushed the box, Cain flipped it back into the house declaring, "You want it? Go get it yourself, Mr. Asshole!"

Wilson shrieked and dove through the opening. Everyone froze, listening intently. The sound of a scuffle was plainly heard by all. Screams, high-pitched and terrified, cut the night air. Then the horrific noises were cut off abruptly by a drawn-out gurgle, followed by total silence.

Cain remarked flippantly, "Sounds to me like poor old fat Sammy just got his throat cut. Who's next?"

Rodney screamed, "There are eight of us! I want that title! Get up there and get it, boys!"

Not one redneck moved a muscle except Rodney who tried to push a three-hundred-pounder up the steps. Jumbo refused to budge, and Cain laughed loudly then quipped in a fake English accent, "Trouble in Redneckville, Rodney old boy?"

Rodney screamed, beside himself with anger, "You chicken shits! Move, damn you!"

Cain couldn't help but needle Rodney, even after all these years, it was still so much fun. "Hey Bro, if you want that title so badly, go get it yourself. Or are you the chicken? C l u c k, C l u c k."

Rodney showed his true color, yellow, but he hid behind his true love, green, his response mirroring his true character. "Guy's, I'll give you five hundred bucks apiece, get me that title."

No one budged, although several took swigs of beer.

"A thousand bucks."

Rodney was getting desperate. Several good ole boys started milling about, discussing Rodney's offer.

Cain greatly enjoyed needling Rodney further.

"Hey Rodney, rednecks can't fathom sums like that. Put your offer in terms they can understand. You know, like: I'll give you a six-pack of Budweiser every day for a year."

Rodney, for obvious reasons, couldn't afford to lose to Cain and spouted loudly, "He's making fun of you assholes, fifteen hundred bucks each, in cash, that's my last offer!"

The good ole boys shuffled around, then a gravelly voice from the rear of the group bellowed, "We gonna let this biker scum scare us? Let's get his ass!"

The rednecks started moving slowly forward as they jockeyed for position next to Rodney at the very rear of the drunken mob where they figured they would still get paid but be a lot safer. The same gravelly voice urged them onward. "If we all jump him at once, we'll take him easy."

The voice from the house spoke again, this time its powerful tones carrying to the mob. "Come inside from the porch, that I might offer assistance in ridding our presence of these overly rotund vermin. We can dispatch them easily as they enter the window."

All movement ceased, some of Rodney's cronies stumbling, caught in mid-step. The voice continued, "You have my oath you will not be harmed. You played the game fairly. You won by using your brains. You did a noble deed by returning our property and you have shown your true worth by facing your enemies with cold steel. I pray you to accept my aid."

Rodney started trying to shame his cohorts into attacking, but the majority were not so drunk that they did not want to talk over this addition to the party.

While they conversed in low tones, Cain spoke to the shadowy figure inside the house. "I played the game to spite my brother and to have a little excitement. I tossed your box back for spite, also and I'm facing these pricks because I have no choice. If I thought I could make it to my bike and ride out of here, I would, I guarantee you."

Rodney, upping the ante to two grand apiece, ended Cain's speech. The rednecks were rallying. Cain heard the sound of pull-tabs being popped as some drank more courage.

The voice from inside the house spoke again. "If you speak true, why have you not embraced my aid? Could it be that you like to fight your own battles? I will make you a bargain. I will take my payment in the sustenance we acquire. I will be honored by my people for the acquisition and will only slow your enemies enough to allow you to dispatch them at your own pace."

Cain hopped through the window. "Don't exactly understand you, but I accept your help and your word. We're about to have lots of company!"

The fight felt like it took hours but actually lasted but a few minutes and at the end, only one redneck still stood on the porch, Rodney. The rest had climbed or had been dragged through the window and somehow removed after Cain dropped them to the floor. Cain had been too busy cutting and stabbing to notice how the disappearances occurred, but several times a body being dragged from under his feet had disturbed his fighting.

Rodney, like a stuck record, screamed over and over, "Help! Help!"

Cain, panting heavily, plopped down on the windowsill to catch his breath and enjoy his brother making an absolute ass of himself. In the pale moonlight, Cain could plainly see the blood covering the floor and the total absence of anything in the room except furniture and a slight figure with a sword in each hand.

His benefactor moved so quickly that Cain's eyes had trouble keeping up with him. A sword rose and fell, and Rodney's screams stopped as he crumpled.

Cain's knife disappeared into his back pocket. His .45 slipped into his hand, the safety snapped off and the hammer clicked to full cock. Cain's voice was filled with astonishment. "Why'd you kill Rodney? He wasn't attacking you."

The voice that answered him sounded very tired. "I did not dispatch him. I merely returned peace to our surroundings. His screaming for help was getting on my nerves."

"Where are all the rednecks?" Cain asked.

The voice answered slowly. "I told you I would accept them as my compensation. You owe me nothing. You may depart at your leisure, although we would appreciate your speed. We must clean up and repair the window to the world before someone comes to investigate."

Cain stepped onto the porch. "I better head west. I won't be safe until I'm out of Indiana. My name's Cain. Thanks for your help!"

The figure answered, "I am known as Erick The Quick. I speak with pride. Thank you for your honor. Sam is going to bother us no more. If you would deposit your brother inside, we will be safe and give thanks to you."

Cain stopped moving and asked, his voice filled with too many emotions to count, "What're you going to do with him?"

Before Erick could answer, Rodney staggered to his feet and approached the window screaming, "I'm going to burn this fucking place to the ground!" He shook his fist in Cain's face and then pulled out his cigar lighter.

Erick grabbed him by the throat, lifted him through the opening, and threw him across the room. The shadows boiled.

Rodney squealed like a stuck pig and then vanished.

Cain started to go to his brother's aid, but Erick suddenly stood in his way and spoke. "I must not allow you to interfere. He has transgressed and must pay. You should leave now so that we may repair the damage and be safe once more."

Cain attempted to raise his gun, but Erick grabbed his wrist in a grip that was unbelivingly strong and stated, "We owe each other nothing. Please leave before we must fight. I will defend my people above all."

Cain snarled, "But he's my brother!"

Erick responded, "I have given my oath of safety to you, and this I shall keep. With your aid, I have gained great stature with my people. Plus, we have acquired, with no further obligations, much meat."

"You mean you're going to eat those fat, beer-soaked assholes?" Cain asked disgustedly, but he never received his answer.

He regained consciousness stretched out on the porch, the perfect expanse of unbroken living room window reflecting the sunlight. An EMT was checking his vitals and the sheriff was ranting about going through the house again and finding nothing. Cain had a baseball-sized knot on his head and a headache larger than the sheriff's belly, which was huge. Three weeks later, he was finally released from jail because the sheriff couldn't figure out what to charge him with. Cain enlisted in the army immediately.

He was on his way to report for basic training and had to ride past the house, so he stopped. The door was locked, but as he looked in the front window, Erick stalked into view. They stood and studied each other silently, then each nodded to the other in mutual respect. Erick opened the window and handed Cain his knife and .45. Cain had questions begging to be asked but remained silent. They shook hands firmly, and then Cain turned away, glad that he had told no one the truth. It was time to get on with his life. He would miss Rodney's games, but not for long. "Special Forces" and "Vietnam" were words that brought excitement just by saying them.

He stood on the porch steps, allowing the sun to bathe his face, listening to the birds, and feeling sorry for his lost brother. Then the image of Rodney, an apple in his mouth, his fat carcass lying on a huge plate surrounded with green veggies, popped into Cain's mind. He couldn't seem to stop himself from exclaiming, "Try clucking now, Rodney!"

The picture would not leave his mind and it produced peals of laughter, especially when someone approached Rodney's carcass with a carving knife and upon it touching flesh, Rodney cut a huge fart. Cain laughed so hard he couldn't breathe and had to sit down for several minutes. After recuperating, he mounted his bike and was still chuckling miles later as he leaned into a sharp corner so far that his bike's kickstand threw multi-colored sparks as it touched the pavement under the fast-moving man and machine.

Goodbye BULLSHIT (BROTHER) and hello future! Of course, as we all now know, being a Vietnam Veteran wasn't much of a future.

Son of a Beech

The huge sprawling tree stuck out of the foothills like a giant leafy mountain. Its dimensions demanded awe but also made its viewers ponder their sanity. Nothing of this magnitude had ever been seen before, and every inch of the planet had supposedly been photographed and cataloged for the last three hundred years. The world government not only advertised but also proved on occasion that no object or person was invisible from its satellites.

The sparkling summer sky set off the tree's dark green leaves and silver-gray bark dramatically, and the three college students stared in wonder and elation.

Shannon squealed, "Wow! You guys ever seen anything this huge? We're going to get an advancement for sure!"

Dru answered while staring. "Yeah, I once saw a very large skyscraper about this size. Though actually, I think it was smaller than this tree. Isn't this tree beautiful? I think it's a Beech tree. I've seen pictures of huge redwood trees, but they were only half this size."

Bob asked in awe, "Dru, where did you see the pictures?"

Dru made a comical face as she answered. "Bob, remember something called Natural History Class?"

Bob grimaced as he wracked his brain. "No, no, not really."

Dru's voice droned on like she was delivering a lecture. "The giant redwoods lost in the fires of 2042. General Grant was the name of the oldest and largest one in Kings Canyon National Park,

California, U.S.A., only a few miles from here."

Bob, as usual, was impressed and embarrassed and his voice reflected both feelings. He questioned jovially, "You ever forget anything in your life, Dru?"

Dru stated flatly, "Not much. I remember almost everything, including the story of the fires that destroyed the trees. The entire state was devastated. Millions of people lost their lives, including some of my ancestors. Lots of strange stories have come out of these hills since. This tree has to be hundreds of years old. Pre-fire, how could the government satellites miss something this huge?"

Shannon interrupted by issuing an order. "Enough bullshit. Bob, take a series of pictures. No one will believe this. I wish we could get the Gravity Sled through the brush, then we could have transmitted video."

Bob wasn't the brightest bulb, but he was an excellent photographer, followed instructions, and wasn't lazy. He pulled his camera out of his backpack, aimed it in the tree's general direction, and pushed the auto button. After the stabilizer light turned green, he left the camera hovering while he stepped several paces to each side to check the angle, then he issued his instructions. "Camera, shoot the entire big tree. Six times."

The camera made six clicking noises then replied, "Pictures acquired, sir."

Bob was planning on shooting some very impressive photos and instructed the camera accordingly. "Camera, switch zoom to 1000X."

Again, the camera responded. "Yes sir."

Bob looked through the camera's viewfinder and exclaimed loudly, "May the Pope marry the Supreme Leader?"

The two girls asked in unison, "What do you see Bob?"

Bob's voice was filled with awe and excitement. "Shit! There's a house and barn by that tree and it looks like they're inhabited."

The two females took turns looking through the camera and had to agree that Bob was right. Dru also noticed a weed-covered trail off to their left which they all agreed their Gravity Sled could negotiate with a little help from Bob. Bob ordered the camera to snap pictures of the house, barn, and grounds, and then they headed for the trail, their sled following Bob obediently.

As they labored up the overgrown path Shannon complained constantly. "Why couldn't we have brought a flyer? Just because we're archeologists doesn't mean we should have to walk. This is so demeaning!"

Dru answered Shannon's question. "The professor hates Bob. That's why we have to walk. We drew him for a partner, so we get to suffer along with him."

Bob's come back sounded miffed and tired. "Look you two, stop blaming me. I know I'm the only man in Archeology 505, but I do have the right to attend you know. Besides, a lot of the ladies like to have me around."

Shannon voiced her opinion in a comical tone. "We do to, Bob, but only at night. You do have to admit though that you should have slept with Professor Dean, then we could have flown in here without breaking so much as a sweat instead of having to hike in with a Gravity Sled as if we were freshmen."

Bob retorted, "Hey! Screw you both! Dean's too old! She has to be at least twenty-five. Besides, I'm the one guiding the dam thing, not you two. It follows me everywhere. Yesterday, it recorded me taking a leak on a tree; the EPA immediately fined me 100 world bills and sent me a five-minute training film on porta-toilets. Either of you want my job?"

Two voices replied simultaneously, "No way, Bob! No way!"

When back in sight of the tree Dru ordered the sled to start transmitting video to the school. The onboard computer stated, "All transmitting systems are jammed. Only recording capability still operational."

Shannon, the tech person on their team, ran every diagnostic she knew to no avail. They discussed returning to the school for repairs but decided that their grades would be adjusted accordingly, so they continued advancing towards the tree, filming everything and making sure to get photographs every few feet.

A wooden fence with a closed gate barred their path, and they stopped to discuss their options. Bob wanted to stop until whoever lived in the house came to give permission and open the gate, but Shannon and Dru outranked and outvoted him. Dru started to open the gate then screamed and pointed. A four-inch spider was sitting on the latch.

Bob told his camera to snap a picture then plucked a rock and was about to squash the spider when he stopped and started laughing. Then he sputtered, "Dru, it's wood."

Dru exclaimed, "What did you say?"

Bob repeated himself. "Your spider's wood. I said it's carved out of wood. Look, will ya!"

Bob and Shannon started laughing hilariously. All three inspected the spider and came to the conclusion that it was the most realistic carving and the largest spider that they had ever seen. They stared at it in amazement. How had anyone carved such minute details into wood? Shannon and Dru opened the gate and Bob moved the sled through, waiting to proceed until they had closed it behind them. They progressed up the trail, stopping to take photos every so often, while the sled's video camera recorded constantly.

As they drew closer to the cabin they heard dull thudding sounds coming from the direction of the tree.

Bob suggested, his voice sounding slightly scared, "Hey girls, let's stop and yell until someone comes. As old as this place looks, the residents might not like us being here and decide to do something about it."

Shannon's answer was extremely rude, not to mention crude. "Shut up, pussy. Dru and I are in charge."

Dru just laughed and nodded her head yes, too occupied by looking at her surroundings to waste time conversing. They continued towards the cabin, the dull thudding sounds becoming louder and more distinct as they drew closer. All three constantly looked upward at the amazing foliage, unable to tear their eyes away.

Shannon tripped over something, looked downward, and stopped dead in her tracks, uttering one word, "Shit!" She stood pointing, her mouth hanging open.

The others froze as they saw what she had tripped over. Everywhere they looked, finely carved wooden statues stood or were strewn about on the ground. Coyotes, cats, chickens, rabbits, cows, pigs, men, women, birds, even several Indians, and a snake or two filled their vision.

As they stood frozen in awe, a voice snapped them back to reality. "What in the hell are you weirdos doing here? Where are you from? Get the Hell out of here before you wind up dead!"

The three stood and stared at the figure doing the yelling. He was old, his skin wrinkled, and he was dressed in clothes that hadn't been available in years. The color and texture of his skin looked remarkably like wood and he was carrying a double-bitted axe, shaking it at them in a very threatening manner.

His next words were even harsher than his first. "Get out of here, you dumbbells! Leave now or join the collection forever. You got maybe fifteen minutes to get on the other side of that gate. You better get your asses moving, or you will stay here forever!" After finishing his rant, he turned and walked slowly to the base of the tree and disappeared around it to the other side.

The dull thumps started again, and Shannon sputtered, "Who in the hell? What did he mean?

Bob, did you get his picture? What do you think we should do?"

Dru, in a very controlled but shaky voice, stated, "Don't know about you! Don't care! I'm getting the hell out of here!"

As she started moving quickly back down the trail towards the gate, Shannon joined her. Bob stood, not moving, hands on his hips and shaking his head no. His loud obnoxious laugh brought the two women to a standstill. They turned to look in his direction and Shannon spouted, "Bob, get your ass and that sled moving. That's an order!"

Bob released a heavy sigh and then calmly stated. "I warned you about coming in here. Remember? Oh, but you two great leaders called me a pussy and ordered me to follow you. Well, guess who the pussies are now? Pictures and an interview would guarantee us the top spot in our class. I'm not leaving here without them. The old man said we had fifteen minutes, you two just wasted five. We can be back out the gate in another five. So, that gives us the remaining five minutes for pictures and an interview. Get your asses moving. You two start interviewing and I'll start shooting. Keep an eye on the clock and move when it's time to go."

Dru and Shannon looked at one another and then all three hurried around the tree. When they got to the other side, the old man was there swinging his axe and cutting into the tree. A huge V-shaped notch had been removed from the trunk in an obvious attempt at cutting the tree down. The old man was working diligently to enlarge and deepen the notch. All around the side of the tree's base, huge mounds of wood chips were piled, many looking old and rotted. Several piles even had large trees growing from them. Trees that had to be very old.

The old man noticed the three and stopped chopping. He turned toward them and bellowed, "What! You three again? Get out of here! Don't you understand English?"

Dru asked politely, "Sir, what's your name? Why are you cutting down this gigantic tree? How long have you lived here? Are you the woodcarver?"

Bob took photos, and Shannon held the recorder.

Dru looked at her watch and remarked, "Three minutes, guys!"

The old man, looking thoughtful, sighed deeply. Then for some reason started answering Dru's questions. "My name is Mark Fullberg. This tree has to die so that all the wooden statues can live again. It survives by draining the life force from all living things, turning them into wooden-looking statues. I have been cutting on this tree for almost two hundred years. When it dies, all the statues will regain their life force and live again. And if you do not leave now you will join the menagerie. Three more statues to bother my conscience."

Bob asked flippantly, "Seeing a shrink, are we?"

The old man had a puzzled look on his face as he asked, "What's a shrink?"

Before Bob could summon some smart-assed retort, Shannon spoke. "It's time! Guys, we have to leave now! Thank you, Mr. Fullberg. We will be seeing you some time in the future."

All three students headed for the gate as fast as they could. Mr. Fullberg didn't say another word, he just stood and watched them go.

After the gate closed behind them, Bob started swearing. "Shit, Damn, Damn this to Hell. I'm going back!"

Dru just stood and stared for several seconds then shook her head no.

Shannon started screaming at Bob. "You idiot! Why would you go back? We've got film, pictures, and recordings. That's all we need. Let someone else risk their life. I'm sure the government can force a number of scientists to volunteer."

Bob was in no mood to argue. He snarled, "You two females always act like you're better than me.

Do whatever you want, when you want. Just stop telling me what to do! I'm going back to talk to that old man and figure out what's going on. If nothing else, all those carved figures are worth millions and I could sure use some of that money."

The three started arguing over the sled and its recordings. The two women pointed out to Bob that if he didn't return, no one would come to help him unless they had proof of what had happened. In the end, the three finally agreed that the girls would take the sled and contents and that Bob would keep his camera and the tape recorder. The girls also agreed that the credit would be split three ways no matter what happened and that they would wait fifteen minutes for him to return before leaving.

Bob slipped through the gate and slammed it shut behind him. When the latch locked, the wooden spider fell to the ground and was retrieved by Shannon. She placed it in the sled carefully, and Dru clapped her hands.

Bob yelled at them, "Hey you two, don't forget one-third of that spider is mine!"

Dru stated, "Only if you make it back alive, asshole."

Shannon looked in Bob's direction, laughed loudly, and gave him the finger.

The girls decided to move farther away from the gate, just for safety's sake, then turned and watched Bob intently as he started back up the trail towards the tree. Halfway there he started slowing down. His steps became erratic and he finally slowed to a stop.

Dru screamed, "Shannon! Look at him! He just turned to wood! Do you think the video recorder caught it?"

Shannon was stuttering with emotion. She screamed back at Dru with everything she could muster. "You cold-blooded bitch! Is that all you care about? What about Bob? He's dead!"

The two milled around for several minutes, then headed back to the school at top speed, followed by Bob's sled. They had to tell someone. They had to get Bob help. Upon arrival, they notified the Dean about what had happened to Bob. No one believed them until after viewing the film and fondling one exquisitely carved spider which was supposedly alive at some time in the past but was now dead and wooden.

The Dean called in the World Police who questioned the girls mercilessly, laughed at them numerous times, and even threatened to arrest them for fraud. The cops only changed their tune after their laboratory reviewed the film of Bob turning into wood and said that it had not been tampered with. The same lab went bonkers over the spider and informed the cops that it had to be formerly alive. As they had never seen tools that could do that fine of work, let alone someone with hands that were steady enough. The cops finally agreed that they would have to go into the hills and investigate.

They left it up to Shannon and Dru to decide

which one would be their guide. The decision was settled by flipping a World Currency Coin.

Shannon lost, her first comment being, "Hey you, Cops! We are flying, right?"

To her dismay, she found out they were driving. Over fifty people were going, all with different disciplines and all with equipment and supplies. They arrived at the foothills in vehicles so large they could not enter the trail. These days even jeeps were the size of small houses.

Shannon tried to warn them, but you know how it is with government employees, they always know more than you, until they're proven wrong. Then it's always your fault. All fifty-one people were forced to march up the trail to the gate carrying their supplies and equipment. Shannon hadn't heard that much foul language in all her life, in fact, she figured that she had probably learned quite a few new swear words during the trek.

Upon arrival, the two cops started surveilling

the tree, house, and barn with binoculars while the technicians set up camp and their equipment. The old man stood, axe in hand watching them from the base of the tree. After much discussion and many arguments, the cops decided to enter and arrest the old man for exhibiting a threatening behavior.

Shannon tried her best to warn them of the consequences, but, as usual, no one would listen.

The cops entered, followed by a crowd of scientists, leaving the gate wide open. The cops rushed the poor old man, grabbed his axe, tackled him, cuffed him, and then drug him by his feet back through the gate, laughing the entire time. Shannon tried to intervene on his behalf and was slapped across the face by one of the cops so hard that she was knocked to the ground. She sat, nursing her bloody mouth, and watched the cops try to force the old guy to answer their questions. When he refused, they kicked him until he passed out.

Shannon burst into tears and crawled over to the old man's side. To her surprise, his eyes opened and he smiled at her. His voice was so faint that she had to place her ear almost against his mouth to hear his words. "Thank you, for caring! Don't worry. These assholes are about to receive their comeuppance; they're about to meet A Beech."

Before Shannon could utter a response, screaming voices reverberated in her ears. "They're all turning into wood! They're all dying!" Most of the voices were unintelligible, but Shannon got their drift. She turned towards the gate and saw the crowd milling and pointing at their fellow scientists who had entered the enclosure. They had all turned into wooden statues.

Behind Shannon came a series of grunts and a very hot nasty smell. She turned back and saw the old man struggle to his feet, smile in her direction, turn bright red, and explode. It was a very strange explosion. No sound, no force, just rings of a brown dust emanating from his body and flowing outwards. It seemed to pass around Shannon into the crowd at the gate. Whomever it touched turned immediately into a statue. In an extremely short time, she was the only live human present; the old man had disintegrated into nothing.

That was Shannon's last memory until she regained consciousness standing by the tree. She stood and marveled as she watched the tree repair the damage that had been done by the old man's axe. The wedge-shaped notch was filled in layer by layer until she could not discern where it had been. At the same time, two large growths were splitting open like a pair of cocoons. The first opened to eject a spitting image of the old man, but much younger. The second scared the hell out of Shannon. It revealed a figure that was her mirror image.

As she stared at herself, suddenly her vision blinked black, and she found herself looking in the opposite direction at herself dissolving. A voice in her head spoke. "Shannon, I am A Beech, your savior. I have never had a daughter before, only a son. Welcome to my family."

Shannon started to freak out but was calmed by the male figure grabbing her hands. He talked calmly as if this happened every day. "Shannon! I'm Mark. This is going to be wonderful. We will live forever. Our dad, A Beech, will care for us and keep the world at bay. In my former life, for some reason I'll never understand, I tried to kill him. But he has forgiven me and placed you here so that I may have company. We are a part of him and therefore need the same sustenance that he does. I will show you what to do."

The next weeks were filled with the work that old man Mark had refused to do. Collecting the remains of the living (statues) and throwing them over the fence where A Beech promptly disintegrated them. Shannon became depressed. Mark kept telling her that it usually wouldn't be this bad. He had refused to do it for quite a few years and the number of statues had piled up. They all had to go, it was hard enough to coax animals into the killing zone, let alone humans when the statues lying around scared the hell out of them. Shannon got Mark to remove Bob, telling him she just couldn't bring herself to do it.

The next batch of cops showed up. Mark and Shannon hid. The first thing the cops did was to inspect the vehicles left by the first group, then the supplies and equipment strewn around just outside the gate. After finding nothing, all nine of them gathered at the gate to discuss what they would do next.

Shannon, peeking at them from her hiding place, exclaimed to Mark, "That's Dru down there, the fourth from the left. We have to stop her from coming in here!"

Mark answered in a whisper. "Not much we can do. Anyone who comes in is a meal. Your group fed A Beech enough life force to repair himself and create us, but we also need to eat, you know. We have been living on squirrels and coyotes with a crow or two tossed in for a week now. To me, these stupid dipshits look like a banquet."

Shannon, switching her attention from Mark back to the group at the gate, spouted, "Mark they're all coming in. What do we do?"

Mark's answer sent a chill down Shannon's spine. "We delay them for a while, then A Beech eats them, and we get our share."

Shannon and Mark had little to do with the cops sticking around the required time. By the time the nine victims were through investigating the house and barn, their time had run out. One after the other, they slowed, stopped, and became rigid. A Beech's words flashed through Shannon's mind. "Get busy. Remove these meal containers as soon as possible, and I will turn them to dust. More will come to investigate and will be easier to lull into our grasp without the containers present."

Shannon and Mark did as ordered. As they

worked, Mark spoke of better things to come. "This is going to make our lives so much easier. These idiots are going to keep arriving and A Beech, you, and I will keep dining on them. WOW! This is going to be great."

Shannon couldn't help but be the rain on his parade. "Have you or A Beech thought about the number of vehicles parked at the foot of the trail? We should pray someone steals some, or the government might decide we are too dangerous and stop investigating and bomb us out of existence."

A Beech interrupted. "I'll think of something, I promise you."

After the remains were taken care of, Shannon stood with her hands against A Beech and absorbed her sustaining life force. She found herself thinking of her future and was definitely not happy. She asked A Beech, "What happens to me if you die? Can I absorb life force on my own or do I die also?"

Her answer was unexpected and came after a long pause. "Shannon, my death would bother you not. If you lay hands on any living creature, you will siphon their life force into yourself. Thereby prolonging your existence."

Shannon was elated. She thought long and hard, then asked another important question. "Why can't we leave the confines of the fence? If we could, it would make the obtaining of food much easier."

This time, A Beech's answer was just plain thrilling. "The fenced area denotes the distance that I can control. I may obviously not leave this area due to physical restraints. Mark may not leave due to the fact that I created him here. But you Shannon, may leave. I didn't create you, I just transferred your life force to a vessel of my creation. I have been considering the vehicle problem that you brought to my attention. I want you to remove them. That is why I answered your questions. You had to know in order to fulfill this task."

Shannon walked around A Beech for several minutes pondering this new revelation. She passed Mark's axe lying on the ground and picked it up, carrying it with her. After a few more revolutions she spoke to A Beech. "I can leave, you can't stop me, and I won't die. Why should I help you? I can go anywhere and do whatever I want."

A Beech sounded very angry, his voice echoing in her mind. "Have you no gratitude? You will live forever as long as you imbibe life force. I demand that you treat me with the respect I am due and do what I request of you! Also, remember that any living thing that you touch will die."

Before Shannon could think of her response, Mark came around the tree. She had no idea what A Beech said to him but he charged her. Her response shocked her and A Beech. She removed Mark's head with the axe without even thinking about it. Then, with no hesitation, she placed her hands properly and ate Mark's life force.

Afterward, she exclaimed, "Holy shit! That felt great. A Beech, screw you, I'm gone. I didn't ask for this, but since I'm stuck with it, I am about to become the world's greatest wood carver. I'll do you one last favor and remove Mark's container. I hope the next flunky you create is better equipped to cut you down. I only wish I could supply him with a chainsaw."

Shannon stood frozen, thinking, then burst into laughter. "I bet this will be the first time that a daughter of A Beech is also a Son of A Beech." She was still laughing as she reached the victims' vehicles.

As she walked past the long line of jeeps and trucks, a man wearing a military uniform popped out of a jeep, grabbed her arm, and exclaimed, "We have to get the hell out of here, lady. The bombers will be here in ten minutes. I have a jeep ready to go up in the front. I was watching with my binoculars, and I can't believe you're still alive. I called in a white phosphorous strike. This entire area will burn. Run!"

Shannon didn't hesitate. The military man became her first carving and he tasted even better than Mark. She found the jeep he had mentioned and drove as fast as she could manage on the rough trail. She wanted to get back to town to start her new carving career. She had to hurry because there were several people at college that she planned to invite to dinner. Although, maybe she should start with some dogs or cats or something smaller as to not draw attention to herself. Not to mention that having something to sell would get her carving career off the ground.

Her thoughts were interrupted by a huge blast of hot burning air striking the jeep. The jeep exploded, and Shannon was thrown into the air, landing in a ditch. There wasn't much of her left, mainly her skull and pieces of her body strewn around. She lay there for a considerable time when a group of buzzards swooped in to feast on her burnt flesh. As she crawled back onto the trail, she made sure to turn the buzzard's statues into dust. She certainly needed something larger than a flock of birds to replenish herself, although their energy had allowed her to reassemble her body parts.

Town was a long way off, but she was sure that she could make it. A gray squirrel bit the dust, after all, every little bit helps. She was sorry that she was unable to carry his statue back to town. Bet she could get several hundred dollars for it. The government had been complaining about the overpopulation of California for at least ten years. Shannon was about to correct that little problem. She was starving.

The Two-Timer

C abot rolled over, groaned softly, then muttered, "Damn, that hurts."

Carefully, he rubbed the bandage on his left bicep. Yesterday the bullet wound had only burned, but today it throbbed with an intensity that was difficult to ignore. Without conscious thought, his hand moved to caress the revolver under his pillow while his mind tuned itself to his surroundings. Each sound was isolated and studied until it was positively identified. The slight snore of his wife, Pat, was easy, as was the wind rustling the leaves in the trees around the tent. Noises were abundant and the softest and the last to be recognized was the scratching of a small rodent's claws as it scrambled up a rock almost thirty feet away. All sounds were declared natural; his world was safe.

He checked his clock, the amount and angle of the predawn light filtering through the tent flaps. Six-thirty, give or take a bit. He relaxed, lulled by the low moan of the morning breeze as it moved steadily up the mountainside, using the pine trees like the reeds of a gigantic flute. That beautiful but somewhat mournful sound could always put him back to sleep, but not today. Summer was almost over.

He sat up slowly as not to disturb his wife then studied her face. She was beautiful, her expression relaxed and contented. He eased out of bed and grabbed his clothes, then slipped through the tent flap, pulled on his Levi's and boots, and deftly tossed his gun belt around his hips. The McCormick holsters slid into position, and Cabot buckled first the belt and then both tie-down straps. He flexed his fingers, dropped his hands to his sides, and like magic, the .45 caliber Ruger Vaqueros appeared in his hands, cocked and ready. He eased down the hammers then twirled the pistols back into their holsters and murmured to a passing fox.

"Not bad for an old fart, huh? Actually, I guess, in my case, not bad for a very old fart."

For the next thirty minutes, from every position imaginable, he practiced drawing his right-hand revolver. He always ended each draw with a flourish. First, roll the pistol forward, then backflip it into the holster. As usual, he finished with a few border rolls, then switched and copied the same routine with his left hand.

"Damn!" he exclaimed. "That hurts."

He was massaging his left shoulder when he smelled Pat's perfume and kidded her. "Trying to sneak up on me, Fuzzy? You forgot to check the direction of the breeze."

Her tone was serious. "The air always moves up

the mountain in the morning, my dear; I didn't want to scare ya and get shot. How's your arm?"

He tried to sound pleasant. "Really sore. That damn bullet cut some muscle. I can still shoot lefty though, don't worry. Did I wake you?"

She responded, "No. Why are you up so early?"

"Couldn't sleep. Going to watch the sunrise from my rock. Want to come?" he asked nonchalantly.

She giggled. "Guess not. You are one weird man though. Besides, that was my rock until I met you."

"You gave it to me, and in case you haven't noticed you're weirder than I am." He really enjoyed kidding her. She tried to make a comical face as she asked, "Why am I so weird?"

"Because you married me," he stated in an unemotional tone then burst into laughter.

"Good point! Go sit on my rock. I'll yell when breakfast is ready."

She was ready to get back to normal, but he

wasn't. "Give me a kiss, woman!" he demanded.

Pat's kiss was long and hard and would have made a Frenchman blush. She almost succeeded in her attempt to coax Cabot back into the tent, but he broke away declaring, "Fuzzy, boy this mountain air sure makes you horny. I'm an injured man. After breakfast, I promise."

She was having trouble talking and laughing at the same time but managed to say, "Promises, promises. Please don't fall off your rock or get shot in a portion of your anatomy that I like a lot, my dear."

Cabot chuckled the entire way to the outcropping known as his or her rock. He sat silently and watched as the sun finished peeking over the eastern mountains, and the sky turned blood red slashed with the vivid contrast of thin stark white clouds. Gradually, the clouds turned pink, then became darker, and finally appeared to bleed. He watched, entranced until the red had dispersed and the sky turned a beautiful yellowish-orange dotted with fluffy white clouds edged in pure gold. In awe of nature's spectacle, he sat unmoving, picking out shapes in the clouds. A buffalo, a rabbit, and a draft horse were easy to identify. One cloud in particular took his fancy. Two people having sex was his final decision and just imagining him and Pat doing their thing put him into a certain mood which was interrupted by Pat's mellow, sexy voice.

"Hey Cabot, breakfast's ready. And so is desert."

He hated to stop interpreting the clouds, but he was starved. Besides, he had a promise to keep and that cloud had given him incentive. Pat was a great cook and after a breakfast of six scrambled eggs and a side order of venison, washed down with cool spring water, Cabot started fondling certain portions of his wife's anatomy.

She spoke intermittently during very heavy breathing. "Hey, stop that. Those are private property."

"I promised you after breakfast, Fuzz! Besides, I saw this cloud—"

Pat cut him off. "Well, maybe I'm not in the mood now."

Cabot yawned, grinned, and then stated, "OK, sorry to have bothered you. I really felt like a nap anyway."

Pat jumped on him, giggling like a little girl. She was certainly in a randy mood, and he was more than willing. By the time their mattress match was finished, it was lunchtime and she fried more venison while he watched, a lustful look on his face.

"Fuzzy, you keep sticking your butt up like that and we're not going to do any work today at all."

"You shouldn't anyway, dear. Let's take the day off and let that arm mend."

She looked at him with those big green eyes, like a deer just before the bullet hit, and Cabot knew that every time he left she worried herself sick that he would not return.

"Fuzz, my arm was an accident. I had that jerk cold. I just didn't think he'd shoot. I haven't been hurt in a long time and you know it. Don't worry, I can still take care of myself."

Cabot's voice was supposed to be reassuring, but Pat replied with facts. "Five years, three months, and twelve days ago, you dragged yourself out of that gully, shot through the chest. Remember? Not to mention how we met. What was it that time? Oh yeah, seven assorted bullet and arrow wounds, huh? And in between? Knife wounds, various traumas from blunt objects, and we won't try to count the broken bones."

Cabot tried to calm her, speaking with humor and using common sense. "Was my lucky day when those Indians chased me up the mountain. Met you, got nursed, got laid numerous times, then married, and I've lived happily ever since. The rest, on-the-job injuries; everyone falls off their horse once in a while, Hon, and you know it."

Pat's next words emphasized her emotional state. "Listen! We have enough. We're rich, Cabot, we don't need any more. You're only doing it for the fun and it's going to get ya killed."

Pat turned her back, and Cabot knew there were tears on her cheeks. He placed his hand tenderly on her shoulder. "Fuzzy, I'll not go today. I'll only carry up what I have stashed with Hi. I wish my damn horse could make it up here. One more trip and we'll pack up and go home. I promise, OK?"

She nodded and then concentrated on the meat in the skillet, keeping her face averted.

Cabot knew her well enough to let her alone and walked over to a large pile of plunder strewn haphazardly by a tree. He stared at the guns, spurs, knives, whisky bottles, boots, and assorted other stuff and stirred them with the toe of his boot, muttering, "Pat, I wish I could take you with me, then you might understand. It's what I do! It's what I am!"

From right behind him came her soft voice. "I

really wish I could go with you, and I know you can't stop. I love you too much to try and make you, but remember, if you get killed, I can't even come to claim your body!"

A long hush that stretched into minutes, broken only by a squirrel as it chattered its disapproval of a coyote passing nearby, was finally ended by Pat murmuring, "Lunch is ready, dear."

They ate in a strained silence. After Cabot helped her with the dishes, he prepared. He cleaned his Rugers then picked his backup weapons. He decided on a .45 Long Colt Winchester rifle because it was light and could throw a lot of lead accurately and quickly. A knife in his left boot and a .25 caliber Berretta in the right and he was equipped with what he considered minimal armament.

Pat found their gloves and waited patiently.

Cabot stated, "Let's go, Fuzz. I hate carrying stuff up the mountain."

She returned tersely, "Let it stay down there

then!"

They strolled along slowly, holding hands until they reached his rock; she could go no further. Cabot kissed her and continued by himself. As always, once past that rock, his stomach became queasy and his heart pounded madly. Going down he always became ill, coming back up did not seem to bother him. Upon reaching the bottom of the gully, he paused to allow his nausea to pass.

Something was wrong! He could feel it. His sickness forgotten, his mind snapped to full alert. He froze. A buck fly droned past, its buzz unmistakable in the still mountain air. A woodpecker pounded on a dead pine just over his head. Ratta-tat-tat. Up gully a quail called, its beautiful song mellow and soothing. A red squirrel started to chatter excitedly, cut off by a scream that echoed through the brush. Even before the first shriek's echoes had stopped, a second ripped at Cabot's eardrums. Cabot, his face a mask of concentration, started to glide forward, his eyes and ears looking for anything amiss.

Unable to see through the brush, he processed the shriek's tones and eliminated the only possible natural source: a mountain lion. His mind then cataloged the cry as both human and female.

"Fun, fun, fun," slipped from his lips as he started to do what he did best, hunt dangerous quarry! He stalked from the gully with an eerie silence, ghostlike, making not the slightest sound, disturbing not so much as a speck of dust. As he came into sight of the first large trees, he could hear voices, garbled at first, then becoming understandable.

A female voice with a heavy oriental accent pleaded, "Peas do not hang my fafer! He did nofing."

A gruff male voice promised, "We'll take care of you again, honey, when we're done hanging the old chink."

Unable to see, Cabot stopped at the edge of

the brush and listened intently, pinpointing three antagonists plus the old man and his daughter. He propped his Winchester against the trunk of a Manzanita tree, removed the hammer thongs from both his revolvers, and loosened them in their holsters. He made a fist with his left hand then massaged his painful arm. Now speed was essential, maybe more than he could muster. He had no way to know his opponent's skills or their armament; he would have to find out the hard way. His spirit and adrenaline soared. Wasn't it great to be alive? It was time for the fun to commence.

He moved forward quickly, absorbing details as soon as his vision was unobstructed. Off to his right, Hi, the old oriental man who tended Cabot's horse, stood on a rock with a rope around his neck. Lee, his daughter, her clothing torn and stained, was on her knees, sobbing. Off to Cabot's left front, stood three scroungy-looking characters sharing a jug and oblivious to his presence. He scrutinized their weapons quickly—only handguns. Old cap-and-ball shit. No holsters either, just stuck in their belts. That would help even the odds a little in his favor. Maybe they were drunk; that would help even more. Three-to-one was usually a safe bet but today, with a bum arm, it could be dicey.

He could hear their horses milling and could only hope that if there was a fourth man, he would be slow to react.

Cabot set his stance, cleared his throat, and the three snapped around to face him. Their faces showed no alarm and they quickly separated. They appeared sober and moved as if they had done this before and had all the time in the world. One slowly removed his gloves, careful to keep his hands away from his gun.

Cabot asked, "What's up, assholes?"

"Who are you?" demanded the man to the far right.

Cabot sneered as he huffed, "The old man and

his girl call me boss. Everyone else calls me Cabot. You three can call me long-distance from hell in just about three bullets time."

"What do you mean?" the same guy demanded.

Cabot shook his head slowly before answering. "You're about to die. That's easy to understand, isn't it? Or are you that stupid?"

The talker looked at his cohorts and licked his lips. The two did slight nods in return. Evidently, they had been in similar situations and had established signals.

Cabot readied himself. Three hands slowly edged closer to their guns.

"Want a drink?" the talker asked as he nudged the jug towards Cabot with the toe of his boot.

The three made their moves in unison. As soon as the "k" sound of the word drink was uttered, the three went for their weapons.

Cabot, his reflexes pumped to the max, not distracted by the jug joke, drew. His right hand pulled a Vaquero and aimed it at his rightmost target. The gun fired, and at exactly the same time, his left hand mirrored the right on the leftmost target. Then in a flash, both guns discharged on the middle target simultaneously. A forward roll and a backward flip and the guns were holstered again, well before the first body slammed to the ground.

Four shots, three targets, one slightly extended bang. His opponents lay, two with dime-sized holes in their foreheads, one with two holes, their brains scattered in funnel-shaped messes to their heads' rear. Before the last body disturbed the dirt, Cabot had slid back into the brush, grabbed his Winchester, and moved rapidly to his right. He dove under a large bush and crawled forward until he could see into the clearing again.

He froze, his eyeballs his only moving parts. He watched as Lee removed the rope from around her father's neck then freed his hands. Belying her frail appearance, she carried her dad to the right side of the rock and crouched over him protectively.

Cabot concentrated on the brush to their left. A buck fly landed on his ear and munched. Despite the pain, Cabot didn't flinch. Sweat ran down his forehead and into his left eye, he only blinked. Minutes passed. Forty yards away, a bush wiggled and a minute plume of disturbed dust drifted into the air. A bird started to alight and at the last minute changed its mind. Cabot finally made out the hazy outline of his quarry. The Winchester spat three bullets, all three explosions so close together that they made one long discharge. The shots were spaced four inches apart with the middle one slightly lower. Cabot rolled to his left and froze again. The bush into which he had fired shook violently, then became still.

Cabot waited with the patience of a snake. After a considerable time, he slipped around the clearing to the horses, counting five. His stallion, Scar, came to the fence and demanded attention; Cabot cuffed him on the nose gently. The other four horses were strangers and ignored him.

Satisfied that he had faced only four opponents, Cabot went to check on the last. Dead was not an adequate description. The man had been lying prone with his shoulders slightly raised, sighting over the sights of a .50 caliber Sharps buffalo gun. Cabot's first slug had entered the left shoulder and exited the lower back. The second had punched through the breastbone and had removed the spine between the shoulder blades. And the third was a twin to the first, only on the opposite side. All three exit wounds were the size of Cabot's fist, which was quite large.

He went to check on Lee and Hi. "You guys, okay?"

Lee answered him. "Yeth, boss."

"Good, sure glad I got here when I did." Cabot was relieved and his voice showed it. He kind of liked these two Chinese people. The old man stood and bowed. Cabot bowed back. Lee shyly smiled, her gratitude evident.

"Only was four, right?" Cabot held up four

fingers to emphasize his question.

They both nodded. While Cabot reloaded, Lee spoke to her dad in Chinese. Her dad's head bobbed, and she said, "Boss, we go get wheel barrel and put tem in hole, tey stink soon if we don't."

"Whatever, Lee, I did my part. I kill, you bury, I pay."

Cabot was relieved that they didn't expect him to help. Cabot killed but never buried, it was one of his rules. The father and daughter left to get their wheelbarrow, and Cabot had to grin. They left the clearing in single file, the dad in front, the daughter behind, just like a little duckling following the parent.

Pat would be worried, so Cabot got busy. He stripped the bodies. All four had several gold coins in their pockets, and Cabot placed them in a pile. The rest of their belongings he threw on a blanket and made into a bundle. When the oriental duo returned with their version of a hearse, or garbage truck, depending on how you classed the dead,

Cabot gave them the coins and told them that the four horses and saddles were theirs also. They could do with them what they wanted. They thanked him profusely, invited him for a sip of tea, and were genuinely disappointed when he explained that he was late and had to leave.

He did his best to run up the mountain, and by the time he arrived at the rock, he was winded. Pat sounded desperate. "Where have you been? Why are your clothes so dirty? What have you got in that bundle? I thought all you had to carry up were more bottles and stuff. Wha...."

"Just a minute, Fuzzy. Shit, let me catch my breath," Cabot gasped.

But Pat finished her questions anyway. "OK! Are you OK?"

He nodded and hugged her. Pat kissed him on the cheek since he was still gasping for air then waited until he caught his breath. She demanded, "Well? Spit it out, Cabot. What kept you?"

Cabot's answer, while not quite the truth, was

also not quite a lie. "I had to help Hi and Lee with a little problem, that's all. I'll go back down and say goodbye and get the other load and we'll pack up and go home. Is that OK with you?"

"What was their problem, Cabot?" Pat was not letting this go, she knew Cabot too well.

"Nothing much, Fuzzy." Cabot didn't want to give her any hints.

"WHAT?" she demanded tersely.

Cabot responded hesitantly, "OK, OK, some assholes were trying to hang Hi, that's all. I convinced them not to, and to donate their worldly possessions to us."

"Cabot!" Pat shook her head slowly. "Even after all these years, it's hard to believe what you do."

Cabot spoke quickly in his sexiest voice, "Let's get finished, Fuzzy. I hear the call of our lonely mattress clear down here. Go get the ATV and trailer while I go back down. I won't be long, I guarantee you."

Pat looked at him with a large smile on her face,

and quipped, "I really hate it when you go down there, but I sure do love it when you get back up." She patted his crotch and took off upslope; he took off down.

Three hours later, they had everything at the tent. Supper forgotten, they spent every ounce of energy doing what men and women have lusted after since mankind crawled out of the ooze. It was late the next morning by the time they were up and around, and after a cold meal, they started to pack.

Pat spoke while she worked. "These whisky bottle labels are still perfect. It's funny how some of the glass changes color and some doesn't, huh?"

Cabot answered her cheerfully. "Yep. Those bottles are worth a hundred fifty bucks apiece. With the effects of those four assholes, we're probably going to clear a hundred fifty grand or so. Not a bad summer, Fuzzy, huh? I should have brought up their saddles, but we still have two left from last year."

Pat giggled while she responded, "Yeah Cabot, you do seem to have the habit of accumulating junk."

Cabot burst into laughter then quipped, "I say junk down there; up here we say *expensive antiques.*" They both laughed long and hard. That was an old joke but still funny.

They finished packing their pickup, hooked up the trailer, and loaded their Honda ATV, then stood enjoying the sights and sounds of nature. Fall was here and soon it would snow. They would spend the winter in their expansive log home in a valley they owned, not far from here. Pat would sell the antiques, dreading spring, and Cabot would practice with his guns and wish winter were shorter. Come spring, she would stall and he would fret until they were back on this mountain. Then he would disappear into that gully, and she would sit on his rock praying for his return.

She had married a man who was a two-timer,

divided in two times in more ways than one. With her in the here and now, he was loving and compassionate, but let him enter that doorway to the past by his rock, and he reverted to what he had been born to be back sometime in the 1800s. A very dangerous predator. She had tried but could not enter his other world. It seemed that he alone had the key. So she would always wait and fear, but never regret, that she had married a man that lived in two times.

Cool Hand Spud

Spud stood nonchalantly in the center of the parking lot, quietly watching, seemingly unconcerned. His head cocked like a small puppy's as he listened to the voices of his opponents and numerous surrounding students. His trademark grin widened as someone commented loudly about him looking so cool. His grin, a twin to the same smirk that Paul Newman had worn in the movie *Cool Hand Luke*. Spud had started practicing his version in the middle of the movie and had it perfected before the film ended.

He knew there was an extremely good chance

that he was about to go down permanently, but there were people watching, and being COOL came with a price, a sum that he had been paying gladly for over half of his sixteen years.

The surrounding crowd, as always, was fickle; they just wanted to see blood flow and really didn't care who bled as long as it wasn't them.

The leader of the gang yelled vehemently at his posse amid the jeers and catcalls from the more drunken portion of the onlookers. "Shit, the last time we only had four; this time there's nine of us. He's making us look like a bunch of pussies! What's wrong with you guys?"

The gang members smirked at each other, pretending to be much bolder than they actually felt, drawing courage from their numbers. They stared at Spud with hate-warped faces as the bystanders snickered and called them ball-less chickens, urging them to do something other than stand around with their fingers up their butts. The gang members' anger rapidly escalated. Their rage and embarrassment, enhanced by the amount of beer they had consumed, overpowered their reluctance for a confrontation. They bellowed threats and gestured obscenely at Spud after the onlookers started imitating the sounds of chickens clucking.

These derogatory noises echoed from the surrounding buildings as every bystander clucked at the top of their lungs. That was the last straw the gang could posture no longer. They were forced into action. They circled Spud like a bunch of wild Indians attacking a wagon train. Being urged on by the onlookers who had started pushing and shoving each other, violence became the only thing on the gang members' minds. This time they were going to win, even if it took all nine of them to do it!

Spud watched their actions coolly, his only movement zipping up his leather jacket while from somewhere deep within his inner self, Bernard's childish voice urged, "Run, you idiot!

Run!

Spud rotated slowly to his left, wondering which one of his opponents would grow brave enough to attack first. Then he burst into laughter at his own stupidity, after all, the question was ridiculous. The answer obvious—none would. They would rat-pack him. He had whipped each one individually, some more than once and some who had brought help, but like rats, as a pack, they were dangerous! Spud spoke loudly, "Spud old boy, nine-to-one, I think this time you bit off more than you can chew, but I promise, someone's gonna get hurt, badly!"

Spud's words caused the gang members' rage to explode as if he had thrown gasoline on their fire, and they narrowed their circle about him quickly. Spud waited, his grin daring them to attack, after all, what else could he possibly do, it certainly would not be COOL to run!

His mind flashed back to when he was a kid named Bernard Grainger and some of these same bullies had picked on him mercilessly. His savior had been a neighbor, a weirdo who dressed in jungle fatigues and was shunned by all. Bernard's dad said the neighbor was a soldier in Vietnam, an animal that could snap at any moment, and that Bernard should stay far away from him.

Spud remembered the day they met like it was yesterday. His name was Zippo, and he had changed Bernard's entire life. Bernard had been hiding in his backyard, crying. He was waiting until his parents left for work so they wouldn't find out he was afraid to go to school. Zippo appeared, seemingly from nowhere, and quietly sat until Bernard's tears had subsided.

"Hey, little man." Zippo had a very quiet calming voice that oozed confidence. He asked, "What's your problem?"

For some reason, Bernard unloaded his entire life story while Zippo sat and listened without interrupting once. Zippo never treated Bernard as anything other than an equal, and they became the best of friends.

His advice was extremely memorable, and Spud could still quote it, chapter and verse. Zippo said, "Go back to school, otherwise those bullies win. A little pain never hurt anybody and as many times as you've had your butt kicked you should know that by now. Remember, losing isn't all that bad as long as you learn from it and you get a piece of your opponent. Personally, I like ears. They come off real easy, hurt like hell, and when they dry, they don't take up much room to store as souvenirs. Ah, but remember, judges get real upset at you when you collect them, so forget I mentioned it. Learn to fight, don't become a bully, be COOL, and if you do lose a scrap, just make sure the guy doesn't want to come back for seconds."

Bernard had taken Zippo's advice to heart, but Zippo had helped him in a much more important way. Zippo was the creator of SPUD, and as such, Bernard owed him everything.

"What you need is a new identity, like Captain

America," Zippo had explained. "Now he was a real ninety-pound weakling, but he worked hard and changed into Captain America and became as tough as they come. All your homegrown heroes are basically the same. They have to work at being strong and bad, not like Superman who was born invulnerable. It's not very hard to be Bad and Cool when no one can possibly hurt you. Don't worry, you'll learn fast! You're so thin, you could eat apples through a picket fence and the only things that would touch would be your ears. We're about to change you from being soft to being hard and tough.

"I'll call ya Spud, and when you're Spud, you're a real tough, I-don't-care, COOL kind a guy! Now it'll take some time and hard work to become Spud, so don't get discouraged. Just you think, all this pain and aggravation is training me to become what I am destined to be: Cool-Bad-Spud!"

And it worked. Bernard became Spud. He went back to school, much to the enjoyment of the bullies, and learned to fight, much to their dismay. He worked cleaning up a karate studio in exchange for lessons and applied those lessons in his almost daily battles. He sparred with Zippo on the weekends and learned how to fight dirty from the former Green Beret. Another Zippo quote came to mind.

"Fighting is fun, but it's also serious and dangerous. Fight to win but don't hurt someone needlessly. If you have to kill, then do it! I'd rather be the one arguing in court than the one rotting in a coffin."

Although it seemed to Spud to take a very long time, he learned and learned well. Bernard was banished to a forgotten recess somewhere deep within Spud's mind. Spud almost never lost a fight, and those who did beat him were very reluctant to face a rematch. People stopped picking on him. He was Spud, the coolest and baddest kid in town. On several occasions, even some adults found out that you didn't push around the skinny kid in the big leather jacket unless you wanted to get hurt and humiliated at the same time.

Spud wondered why Zippo named him after a potato and asked. Zippo's answer was odd, to say the least. "Spud is a short, easy-to-remember name. People will make fun of it, but few will forget it! And you have to admit, it is so much better than Bernard." Zippo laughed so long and hard Spud was forced to join in.

The gang interrupted Spud's thoughts. One member charged from the front while others came at him from all sides. Spud slipped into battle mode. Taking them out one at a time was his only alternative, and since the guy in front of him was swinging a beer bottle and slightly closer than the rest, Spud started with him. No time for niceties, he had to thin them out and do it quickly. His left arm blocked the bottle and his right ridge hand struck solidly on the punk's left temple. The guy wilted like a limp noodle, his eyes rolling upward until all that could be seen was white.

Spud started to turn but wasn't quick enough. A shoe hammered the back of his left knee and it popped with a pain so intense that he screamed. The loss of support turned him slightly and as he toppled, another target was presented. He drove his fist into the guy's groin, the impact numbing his arm to the elbow. Whoever he had hit threw up immediately and half-digested pizza and beer showered everyone.

Spud continued falling, unable to cushion himself with either hand because he was busy hitting attackers with both. He inspected the asphalt at close range, the length of his smashed nose, and after he kissed the pavement, everything became blurry as feet, fists, and objects battered him from all directions. He should have curled into a protective ball and given up, but that would not be cool, so instead, he kept fighting. The battle turned frenzied as he connected time after time with his enemies, causing their rage to engulf them completely, their human reasoning giving way to an animalistic fury. Someone's head got a little too close and Spud snatched himself an ear. The resulting high-pitched scream gave Spud a quick warm feeling, and although no one else could hear him over the yelling and cursing, he exclaimed, "Got my first ear! You were right, Zippo, they come off real easy!"

Spud heard the distinctive voice of Randall Tate, gang leader and alpha male, shriek, "He tore my ear off! I'm bleeding like a stuck pig! Kill that son of a bitch!"

The pack paused in their attack momentarily as if the sight of Tate's blood had brought them back to their senses. Spud took advantage of the lull to break one of his opponent's ankles with a well-aimed kick instead of trying to regain his feet. The resulting scream of pain broke the respite, and wailing like banshees, everyone that could still move jumped on Spud like rats on a piece of cheese. Spud did his best to defend himself, but a hard kick to his ribs broke several, making it difficult to breathe, then his left wrist snapped leaving him basically one-handed. Ignoring it all, he fought on, but suddenly, an extremely hard blow landed at the base of his skull. His end of the fight was over, he could still see, hear, and feel, but was no longer able to move.

Within his mind, Bernard's small voice chided, "I warned ya! We're dead."

As the kicking and stomping continued nonstop, Spud decided that living might not be an option. Being COOL and having a bad reputation called for taking chances, but in retrospect, he decided they were not worth getting killed for. Oh well, too late now! Bernard's voice returned. "You'd do it again and you know it. FOOL! Anything to be known as COOL."

Spud wished that good old Bernard would go back into hiding and let him alone. Losing this fight was bad enough without having to listen to his sniveling. The blows to his head increased in intensity as they pretended it was a football and being paralyzed left Spud no choice but to lay there and absorb the punishment. Cheers were the last noises he heard. Oddly enough, he thought one of the cheering voices was that of his own sister giving encouragement to her boyfriend, who now had only one ear.

Dim lights and the fuzzy square pattern of ceiling tiles were what registered vaguely to Spud as he became aware of a heated discussion about how someone had gotten badly injured. A female voice asked, "Is he going to make it, Doctor?"

"It's too early to tell, Nurse." The doctor's voice sounded upset.

"He's sure a mess, Doctor. Do you know what happened to him?" That female voice sure sounded kind and sweet. Spud found himself wishing that he could see her.

The doctor's voice was tight and angry as he answered, "A gang of bikers attacked one of our students and more of the students rescued him. Quite a few were injured. This degenerate got what he deserved. What a waste. Someone should pass a law against motorcycle gangs!"

Spud thought that the doctor's description sounded sort of off but also sort of familiar. He couldn't seem to focus on what the errors were. He felt as if he were lost in fog, fighting his way through a bat of cotton. He tried to listen closer to what was being said and heard the nurse's sweet voice again.

"Hey Doc, I heard it was the other way around?"

Something about that statement made sense to Spud but he still just couldn't quite get his mind wrapped around anything substantial.

"Shut up and get him on the bed, Nurse. And no, the National News got it backward. I talked to the police chief. Besides, why would our students dirty their hands on some biker? Not to mention that we had to pry our quarterback's ear out of this one's hand!"

The doctor sounded like he was getting angrier by the minute and Spud wondered if they were talking about Zippo. He prayed that they weren't! The ear comments were striking a familiar chord but Spud still couldn't seem to focus.

"They sure stomped him good. Look at his head, it's almost flat, yet lumpy. Kind of like a burlap sack full of smashed potatoes."

Spud decided that the nurse could evidently talk as long as she worked at the same time since the doctor didn't complain or threaten her. He tried to ask who they were talking about but couldn't seem to get the words out. He also felt like laughing at the potato reference but couldn't do that either. Their conversation continued with him hanging on every word.

"Yeah, besides his broken bones, he'll lose several fingers on each hand, and if the brain swelling doesn't kill him, it always causes people major problems for the rest of their usually short lives." This time the doctor sounded almost happy.

The nurse started talking again. "Poor kid, he can't be much more than sixteen. We had a patient in long-term care once whose brain had swelled badly. He was in a coma, but his brain still created so much energy that if you got within ten feet of him all the hair on your body would stand on end and vibrate. Freaked me out. They had trouble getting anyone to nurse him at all. I couldn't stand it myself. I pity this poor kid!"

"Nurse, this punk got what he deserved. He might have killed someone." Now the doctor's voice dripped with venom.

Spud decided that he didn't particularly like this guy.

The nurse started up again. "I don't think stuff like this should ever happen, Doc. I think—"

The doctor had reached the end of his patience. "Nurse, shut up and do your job or I'll get someone who can!"

The voices faded away with Spud feeling sorry for the nurse and whomever they had been discussing. That doctor was sure an asshole. Like ninety percent of this town, root for the wealthy, screw everyone else, even if they had to have help to do it. Spud's parents included. They had given up on him when he had bought his first bike.

Zippo had been the only one who had given him any encouragement. "Spud! Always be your own man." Zippo's words had been a little slurred due to an intake of beer. It was Zippo's twenty-first birthday celebration, attended by two, him and Spud, or three if you counted Bernard who still popped up every now and then. In this case to berate Spud for having a brew or two.

"Spud, don't let anyone push you into being something you're not happy with." Zippo had continued after chugging another can of beer. "Don't be like me Spud, whatever happens, don't be like me!"

Zippo never talked about himself and Spud was

so surprised, he didn't know what to do or say, so he just kept handing Zippo beers and listening. Zippo talked between swallows.

"My real name is Ichabod Mercer. Makes Bernard Grainger sound swell, doesn't it? My father wanted me to have a career in the army just like him. I wanted to be an architect, but no, he wouldn't hear of it. So, to keep peace in the family, I gave in. I joined the army at sixteen, my parents joyfully signing their permission. I graduated high school on June 6, 1965, at the top of my class two months before my seventeenth birthday. I was in basic training at Fort Jackson South Carolina three days later.

"Then I went on to Advanced Infantry Training, Survival School, Special Forces Training, and finally the ultimate training classroom in the world, South East Asia, or Nam to ignorant people who didn't have to go. I had done exactly what good old dad wanted, except now he won't even talk to me because I personally, according to him, disgraced our entire family tree by killing babies and losing the war single-handedly.

"An opinion most of this country seems to agree with. Guess Korea was a great military success and politicians never lie! I saw no reason to stay in the army, being such an abject failure before I was even nineteen. All I ever wanted to be was an architect, now I'll never be anything; all I can do is whatever odd jobs someone takes pity on me and allows me to do. Baby killers are not at the top of the hiring lists.

"It seems Vietnam Veterans are all lower than the chicken shits that ran off to Canada or joined the National Guard to keep from being drafted. So I hang out at the local watering hole where the drunks don't seem to care who I am, and every once in a while get to have some fun in a fight. I'll be an embarrassment to my old man till the day he dies, which no one will tell me about, so I'll miss the funeral. But when I'm an old man, I can dream about what could have been if I had gone to college and become an architect, with a little time off in Canada to duck the draft, of course. Until then, I guess I just get to suffer alone. Wonder if my dad would have talked to me then; he seems to be OK with allowing everyone else to come home from Canada with no penalties. Do your own thing Spud, or you'll live to regret it!"

Zippo passed out promptly after making this last declaration, and Spud stayed and kept an eye on him until morning. When Zippo woke up, Spud wanted to ask him a lot of questions, but it became quickly evident that Zippo had no memory of the previous night's conversation.

Spud wished that he could talk to Zippo again, but Zippo had been sent to prison for teaching an off-duty cop some manners. Even the judge admitted the cop was wrong but gave Zippo two years for defacing town property. Guess the judge thought enough people around town had an ear missing and decided to teach Zippo a lesson.

Zippo's only comment had been, "Spud, I'm sorry they made me give that cop his ear back. I should have swallowed it! Glad you never started to collect them yourself like I told you. Judges have no sense of humor."

The next time Spud came to, he was forced to realize that the injured kid was himself. He heard the nurse talking to his parents. "Your son is in a lot of pain. His brain has swelled larger than any that we have ever seen before and they had to cut away sections of his skull to relieve the pressure. Brain damage almost always occurs when this happens. We don't know what type or how much, but we're sure he will never be normal. It does appear, however, that he isn't going to be permanently paralyzed. As soon as the inflammation at the base of his brain shrinks, he should be able to move again. I know that this isn't much, but it's all we know at this time."

Spud's mom shook her head sadly and clucked her tongue while his dad spoke. "I just don't understand why he and his buddies attacked that poor student. Four students with broken bones, one in a coma, one missing an ear, and four others with assorted major injuries. Ah! I have to admit, I guess Bernard got what he deserved!"

They walked away discussing how ashamed of Bernard they were and wondering if some jail time might straighten him out. It was their first and last visit until he was released and they were forced to come and pick him up. His sister never visited him at all!

As his parents walked away, the nurse patted Spud's hand and stated emphatically, "Glad I'm not related to that pair. You poor thing! Hope you didn't hear that."

Spud heard every word, but luckily Bernard must have missed the entire conversation. Once in a while over the next few weeks, he would pop up and sniffle and snuff about the family not visiting, but Spud always managed to bury him again before things got out of hand.

The police came to question Spud often. It seemed that they had a problem, one hundred or so witnesses that had seen the wrong thing: Spud being stomped by a gang of students and him defending himself. A local ATM security camera had even filmed the one-sided fight. Although it had been plainly self-defense on Spud's part, the police were trying to figure out how to charge *him* for the incident.

They surely couldn't put all those students in jail, especially since most of their parents were the crème de la crème of the town. Black eyes, broken bones, and noses aside, they had three students, one of which would speak with a high voice for the rest of his life and never be able to have kids, one who had his ear sewn back on, and the other who was going to do a lifetime imitation of a rutabaga.

Spud said absolutely nothing. He just lay there and listened. He hadn't even heard from Bernard in quite some time. He couldn't believe it, but he almost missed the wimp.

He felt like he was somewhere else, a spectator being forced to observe his life through a window. If Spud hadn't been so COOL he would probably have been babbling for his mommy or thinking of committing suicide like Bernard the last time he had shown up. His head felt as if it was a quart over full and his pain was off the charts. On a scale from one to ten, the agony was about a twenty.

On a good day, Spud felt like a twenty; on a bad day, the number was so high Spud couldn't even fathom it. When anyone came near him, he became cold as ice, a red film covered his vision, and his head sounded like a giant rattlesnake was loose inside, the buzzing so intense at times that it drowned out everything. Talking was something that Spud knew he could do but just didn't feel like doing. Maybe he should have, and then he could have asked for more pain medication.

The police were becoming more and more insistent. Public opinion was being shaped by the local TV station, owned by the parents of the student in the coma. They were twisting the facts while the national media, telling the truth, was holding up the town as a bad example to the rest of the country. All this exposure was putting enormous pressure on the police chief to resolve the problem.

In desperation, he sent three policemen to question Spud and gave them an ultimatum. "Either get a confession from that biker or turn in your badges. And off the record, I really don't care how you do it! Just make this go away! Now get out of here, and this time don't come back empty-handed!"

The three agitated police officers entered Spud's room a short time later while Spud's nurse was checking his vital signs. One humongous officer looked at Spud and declared, "We're here to get answers. Your doctor says he can find no reason why you can't talk. So today, you're going to start."

Two of the cops stood at the foot of Spud's

bed and glared at him while the huge one pushed the nurse out of the way and grabbed Spud by his gown front, lifting him completely off the bed. The cop screamed at Spud, his nose almost touching Spud's. "Listen Punk! I want answers and I want them now!"

The nurse sputtered, "What do you think you're doing? Leave him alone or I'll call security!"

One of the cops from the foot of the bed grabbed her by the arm and stated firmly, "The doctor warned us about you, and if you don't stand there quietly, you're going to have more trouble than you can get out of."

"What do you mean by that? Are you threatening me?" she asked, her voice shaking with rage.

"You're damn right we are, lady! So do us all a favor and forget what you're about to see, and shut up while you're not seeing it!" He stood there and squeezed the poor nurse's arm until she whimpered with pain.

She finally gasped, "OK, OK. Please don't hurt me anymore, and please don't hurt him either. He hasn't said one single word since he was admitted."

The cop holding Spud laughed and shook his massive fist in the nurse's direction to emphasize his threat. "He'll talk today, Nursey, or he's going to be sorry! You think that face of his looks bad now, wait till I get done with it."

Spud's expression remained blank. Bernard started whimpering, but the rattling in Spud's head became severe and drowned everything out, then abruptly stopped as something popped. An intense pain lanced through Spud's brain like a bolt of lightning followed quickly by an almost overwhelming clarity. Thoughts and concepts raced through his mind at blinding speeds and he somehow understood every one of them.

He found that he grasped knowledge that he never knew existed. He was suddenly aware of what he could do and how he could do it. He banished his pain to a small room in his mind and slammed and locked the door forever. His trademark grin returned and the headline, THE SHIT IS ABOUT TO HIT THE FAN! filled his mind like a huge billboard.

The officer still at the foot of the bed remarked, "Look at that kid's eyes. They're as red as beets."

The nurse exclaimed, "Why shouldn't they be? His blood pressure is off the charts. You cops should get out of here and leave him alone before he blows a vein!"

The huge cop's face that held Spud suddenly went stone white, his jaw fell open, and his eyes bulged. He went totally rigid and started drooling as Spud slipped in and took control. Spud looked out of the cop's eyes with awe, focusing on his own face. He felt like he was going to puke. He had never been very handsome, but now he was a sickeningly misshapen and gross-looking freak.

At that moment in time, he realized that he would never be his old cool-looking self again.

Someone, he decided, was going to pay and pay dearly, or actually, they were all going to pay! Every damn one of them!

He looked around, his new vision turning red. He laid his empty shell gently back onto the bed and said quietly, "Don't go anywhere I'll be home in just a minute."

Spud held the cop's massive right fist up before his eyes and flexed the fingers slowly, enjoying immensely the feeling of brute strength it contained. He turned quickly and struck the cop holding the nurse with a vicious backhand to the chin. The nurse staggered as she was freed, but managed to keep her feet as her captor hit the floor moaning.

Spud wasted no time. He spun the big cop's body on its left heel and hammered the last cop in the stomach as hard as he could with a solid right. The cop doubled over with pain and threw up. As Spud turned his new body back around to face the nurse, her former arm twister lurched to his feet unsteadily, holding his jaw in place with both hands and mumbled, "George, what the hell's the matter with you? You broke my jaw!"

Spud reached out with that huge hand and grasped the broken jaw, twisting viciously; the resulting shriek should have been heard for miles. The wail ended as the cop hit the floor semi-conscious. Spud leaned over and whispered into his ear, "You got what you deserved. Next time try twisting a man's arm!"

Spud transferred into the cop with the stomachache and promptly snapped-kicked the huge cop in the head so hard that he propelled him out the door and into the hall. Spud followed him out, planning on thumping on him some more; followed by a piece of advice, but when he saw the dent in the cop's head, Spud decided any further interaction would be useless. The guy was deader than dead.

He spoke through lips that were a lot thicker than his own and in a voice that he couldn't identify with. "What do you know? All that muscle and bulk topped with a skull as thin as an eggshell. I would have never guessed. With a brain as small as his and a body as large, you would have thought he would have a skull as thick as a water buffalo's."

Spud transferred back to himself to watch the aftermath. The nurse stood like a statue in disbelief. Spud was a little sorry that the overly large cop was dead, but not really. After all, the SOB had been ready to beat up a disabled patient in the hospital less than one-third his size and had also condoned threatening and abusing a really nice nurse! Actually, Spud decided that he had done the right thing, and that maybe, just maybe, life might be worth living again.

Then Bernard showed up to ruin the mood. He sniveled, "Look at what you have made me into! I'm ugly and you're a murderer!"

Spud tried to explain that it had been an accident, but Bernard would hear nothing. After all, he had always been pigheaded.

The last cop standing, ignoring his stomachache, stood staring off into space, hyperventilating and shaking like a leaf, seemingly trying to understand what had just happened. After shaking his head like a dog with a tick in its ear for several long moments, he suddenly turned and yelled at the nurse, "Get a doctor!"

The nurse replied caustically, "Get him yourself, asshole."

She checked Spud's pulse and asked politely, "Are you all right, you poor thing?"

She did a double take when Spud calmly replied, "I couldn't be better ma'am. How are you?"

She started to ask him something else but was interrupted by the arrival of the hospital security guards who were attempting to ascertain what happened. They got absolutely nowhere and left very disgruntled. Finally, the dead cop was removed and a doctor patched up the one with the broken jaw.

The police chief arrived and spent ten minutes cussing out everyone involved after getting no story that made any sense to him. He left blaming Spud for all that had happened, and the nurse never informed anyone about Spud being able to speak.

After the room was cleared and they were alone, she asked Spud, "How long have you been able to talk?"

He answered, "A while."

"Are you feeling OK?" she asked.

"Never felt better, ma'am. How's your poor arm?"

She smiled and said, "It's OK. By the way, talk if you want. Don't if you want. That's up to you and it's no one's business but yours. I don't know what happened, but for some reason, I feel as if I should thank you."

"For what? Those cops took care of themselves. What could little old sickly me have to do with anything?" Spud replied, his smile beaming like a lighthouse beacon. "Thank you very much for caring for me! You're a very good nurse and a very nice lady. I'm sure one ugly sucker though, huh?"

She didn't answer him, but after she left, Spud could hear her crying as she walked away down the hall. The next day she informed him that the cop with the broken jaw had been fired for assaulting her and the other cop had been given a commendation for stopping the one who had died from assaulting him. No one seemed overly upset that the cop had died as he was universally hated and well known for being especially brutal. He had been demoted a year or so before for getting into trouble while off duty. Some guy had torn his ear off and that had made him even meaner.

Spud said nothing, just laughed to himself and thought about how small the world was, but Bernard popped up again and between sobs accused Spud. "Hope you're happy! Because of you, I look like some freak out of a circus sideshow, and I'm trapped in here with a killer!"

Spud couldn't argue with him since he was right but managed to get him to go away by promising vengeance for being ugly and to be more careful in the future when he kicked someone in the head. Besides, he hadn't known that cops wear steel-toed shoes. Bernard faded away; he had always been a sucker for a good story. Spud thought about locking the weenie into his room forever but decided that wouldn't be right since technically Bernard had been around longer than him.

Staff visiting Spud's room, especially one doctor in particular, started to have all sorts of accidents, and Spud's grin returned to being a permanent portion of his face. In fact, if anyone who had known him before would have visited him in the hospital that grin would have been the only part they would have recognized.

The nice nurse and her doctor friends were the only visitors who had no problems and they had many long talks about his medical condition. She brought him books on various medical subjects and was amazed that he understood all that he read. His favorite subject was the regeneration of tissue, and she even convinced some of the doctors in the hospital to stop by and discuss their specialties with Spud. Several became regular visitors and were astonished by his knowledge.

His parents reluctantly picked him up upon his release and informed him that as soon as he could walk, he was on his own; they were through being embarrassed by him. Spud returned to school as soon as he could. He was still unable to walk but could handle his wheelchair, although somewhat awkwardly. His fingers were regenerating nicely but were extremely tender, and the gloves he wore to hide them chaffed terribly.

The school had been notified of his return, and the vice principal met him at the bottom of the front door's handicap ramp. "Mr. Grainger, or should I call you Spud? You do look like a mashed potato, especially your head. You certainly won't ever win a beauty contest. Ha, ha. I hope you've had a miserable time. They say you can't talk anymore, but that you can write."

Spud spoke very quietly. "I can talk when I have something to say."

The vice principal sounded like a mad preacher. "Well, whatever, just write this in big letters. Bernard Grainger, mess up just one time and you're out of here! The state is forcing us to let you graduate. You got away with everything by the skin of your teeth. You cost this school by hurting those other students. If there is ever a next time, you won't be so lucky."

Spud sat and stared into the distance, eyes blank, and his grin infuriating. The vice-principle sounded distraught. "Your own parents are ashamed, and every person in town wants a piece of you for what you did. Unfortunately, your fellow gang members have never been located. If the national news hadn't made us look so bad, you'd be buried under the jail. Now get to class, before I personally wipe that smirk off your ugly mug!"

Spud had trouble getting his chair up the ramp. He had not practiced much; he had had other things to concentrate on.

Just as his chair reached the door, the vice principal promptly closed it, saying mockingly, "Grainger, if you're late, you get detention. Ha, ha, ha."

Spud borrowed one of the nerds to open the door, or he would have had to sit there all day. The nerd was still trying to figure out why he had done it when Spud borrowed another to push him down the hall to homeroom.

On the way, Spud passed several students who pointed at him and snickered or made nasty comments about his looks. Everyone else turned away and ignored him completely except a few people who pretended to throw up as he rolled past. He sat in his wheelchair, his grin in place, and ignored everyone. He was forced to hum to himself in order to drown out Bernard's whimpering.

Once in class and safely parked in the back of the room where he could barely hear what the teacher was saying, Spud started. He had spent every waking moment waiting for this opportunity since he had been discharged from the hospital.

A small transparent blob formed in front of his eyes. It took form until it resembled water suspended in space. He could simply have entered the other's body but this way was much cooler and a lot more fun. Spud's grin blazed as the blob wafted its way across the room to a football player who sat in the front row, sound asleep as usual. The globule changed shape rapidly and turned pink. First, it formed a smiley face that turned into a hideous mask, then a hand with the middle finger extended, and finally, a jellyfish shape with long tendrils that slithered into the guy's left ear. The remarkable thing about this glob was that the only person who could see it was Spud, who was having great difficulty keeping from bursting into laughter.

The football player jerked to attention, sucked on his right thumb for several minutes like a newborn, then stood and climbed on top of the teacher's desk. Moving very slowly and deliberately, he dropped first his trousers and then his shorts, then slowly bent and mooned first the class and then the teacher. The teacher tried to get him to quit repeatedly to no avail, and in desperation sent one of the punk faction to get the principal.

The player kept up his mooning amid catcalls about the size of his manhood, jeers, cheers, and an occasional spit wad. Then the principal stormed into the room. The football player stood motionless, right hand wrapped around one butt cheek, his left clutching the other, clothing around his ankles, and his eyes saucer-like. He slowly looked around the room mystified then down at himself and mumbled, "Duh! What... what's going on?"

The principal screamed, "Get down off there, you pervert! What in the Sam Hill are you doing?"

The player had no clue how to answer. He tried to jump off the desk without pulling up his pants, landed in a heap on the wood floor, and started to cry.

The principal rushed to his side, inspected the damage, and declared, "Broken collar bone. You idiot! We have a game Saturday!"

The player rocked and moaned in pain then suddenly turned silent and expressionless and clubbed the principal in the mouth with his good arm.

The principal landed on his back, his mouth bleeding profusely. As he slowly got up, he yelled at the player in a very high-pitched voice, "You're done, Robinson! And I don't care who your old man is or how much money he has or how good you are at football! No one hits me! You're going to jail, and if it's the last thing I ever do, you're not going to graduate either!"

Spud closed his eyes as the scene finished playing out; this kind of enjoyment must be savored. He was glad he had decided not to make every jock and ass-kisser in school go out and play in the middle of a busy freeway during rush hour. That way, one brief moment of terror and their punishment would be over. The long-term approach was definitely going to be more fun. The students who had attacked him and their supporters were about to have some major problems. Bernard's comment made Spud almost lose control and laugh hysterically. "Not bad! At least you didn't kill anyone!"

Sure beats listening to you whine, wimp, and cry all the time, Spud thought.

The head cheerleader did a striptease act in the library; everyone now knew she wore falsies and was definitely not a natural blonde. The vice-principle shut the front door on his left hand

and lost two fingers, then after returning from the hospital, lost another finger on his right hand to a voracious filing cabinet drawer. But the crowning glory of Spud's first day back in school was when his sister carved her initials on Randall Tate's butt with a scalpel in biology class instead of dissecting her frog, which Randall promptly swallowed. The ability to control two people was a milestone in Spud's research and development program.

The accidents and antics at school kept up continually and drew all attention away from Spud and his looks. He was treated as the invisible man. He wished on numerous occasions that he could shout his achievements from the rooftops, but the thought of becoming a government guinea pig, or at the very least, sharing a cell with big Bubba, promptly brought him back to reality every time. Bubba didn't really scare Spud, but the thought of needing to sleep at some point in his incarceration made his butt pucker dramatically.

All such thoughts aside, even Bernard seemed to

be enjoying the payback! His only comments were getting tiresome. They were equally split between "at least you haven't killed any more people" and "don't kick him or her in the head!"

When Spud was able to walk again, his parents rented him a small apartment and sent him an allowance each month to live on. He got their hint and never once returned home. He stayed extremely thin as always, but his misshapen head grew slightly larger and drew stares wherever he went. His mind grew stronger and stronger, and he loved to ride through the town at night changing all the red lights green so he never had to stop. He never missed the Friday night's fun of sauntering across the school parking lot, much to the dismay of his former attackers.

On several occasions, the students had taken physical means to stop Spud, but after two had been sent to the hospital with numerous broken bones, administered by Spud manually, and one group being hit by the town police car, they left him strictly alone.

By the end of the year, the school and town were in turmoil and Spud was as happy as he could be. People were no longer as fanatical about wealth. The town's interest turned to basketball, and Spud, who had no problem with those ball players, minded his own business and kept messing with the guilty. He felt as if he had found his true calling: payback.

One day as he sat in the park discussing his future with the pigeons, he was suddenly interrupted by a woman's screams. "Stop! Help, help!"

He saw two guys in a struggle with a woman over her purse across the park from him and crossed the distance in a flash. By the time he arrived, the two crooks had the woman on the ground. One was pulling on her purse, to which she stubbornly clung, and the other kicked her in the side. Spud threw a heel palm to the nose of the one and elbowed the other in the side of the head.

They both ran.

The woman stammered, "Those punks! Someone should stop them!"

Spud's grin widened and his eyes narrowed. He exclaimed, "You asked for it, lady! You got it!"

The two fleeing criminals were inundated by at least a hundred pigeons. They were pecked, flogged, scratched, dive-bombed, and finally, two pigeons grabbed an ear from each man in their talons and flew off. The two crooks were still screaming for help and bleeding profusely when the police arrived. Spud couldn't help wondering how the judge would blame Zippo for this one!

"Thank you, sir." The woman stared at Spud's head as he helped her to her feet.

"No problem, ma'am. Don't worry, I won't bite you. I know that I look like the elephant man's uglier brother."

She exclaimed hurriedly, "I'm so sorry! I didn't mean anything. Did you see those pigeons?"

Spud giggled then stated, "Oh, that's OK. Yep.

It's a crazy world. Probably mutants. There are things running around this old universe that would curl your hair, or tear an ear off for a souvenir. Ha, ha. You OK?"

"I guess so. Thanks again, sir." She sounded tired.

"No problem. You take care, ma'am." Spud started to walk away but was interrupted by her voice.

"Ah, here, sir." She handed Spud a twenty-dollar bill.

"What's that for?" he asked pointedly.

She answered him in a contrite voice. "It's a reward. Please take it! I could have been hurt. I'm not rich, but I can afford twenty dollars. You saved me. Besides, frankly, you look like you could use it."

Spud's voice mirrored his surprise. "Thank you and you're right, I guess I can use it."

He glanced at his watch. He had to get home and go to work at the hot dog stand. He would sure be glad when he no longer had to play the cripple; the gloves he always wore hid his new fingers, but this role was getting rather tedious. He had managed to regrow his fingers completely. The fingers that he had regenerated on a cellular level were a little longer than his others but were twice as strong and much more flexible. When he had first discovered his new abilities, they had cost him every ounce of energy that he possessed to use. Now he could use them without breaking a sweat, and he discovered a new ability almost every day.

Of course, his real challenges were to keep from getting caught and becoming a government science project, or bursting into laughter at some of his own antics. Luckily, graduation was only two weeks away and after turning it into a very memorable occasion, he could leave town and get on with his life. He wanted to explore a little because on several instances he had bumped into another mind much like his own. The contact had been brief, and whoever it had been with had recoiled so quickly that Spud had been taken by surprise. Every now and then he got the distinct feeling that someone was watching him, but had always written off the feeling as paranoia.

He felt the pressure on his mind again and reached out. A split second and he realized that the other mind was female and in close proximity.

He heard a sexy drawl. "Hi, I'm Constance. Don't panic, you can't see me. I'm uglier than you are. I'll show myself if you promise not to puke or scream or something!"

She talked so fast that Spud had to think through what had been said before he could reply, "Ahm, I promise."

"OK, here I come. Oh, should I come fast or maybe just fade in?"

Spud decided on fast and told her, "Fast, otherwise people are going to notice."

POP! She appeared. Spud stared. She was a little shorter than him and very well built, wearing tight jeans and a low-cut sweater. He was still staring when she stated hotly, "You don't have to stare. I got shot in the head by a 12-gauge shotgun loaded with what they call shredders. You know, what the cops use to blow down doors. Miracle I lived, or so they say!"

"I hadn't noticed," Spud stammered.

She asked quickly, "Then why are you staring?"

"Your sweater fits real snug, and if you don't want me to stare, stop sticking your chest out and cover it up."

A silence followed Spud's statement in which he finally looked at her face. It was a mess, in fact, her whole head looked like a jigsaw puzzle that someone had forced the pieces together all wrong then sewed or stapled them into place leaving angry-looking red, swollen, bumpy seams. Her face was bright red, and it took a while for Spud to realize that she was blushing.

He asked her, "Why did someone do that to you?"

She responded, "It's a long boring story about an alcoholic cop father and a mother with real loose morals and getting caught standing between them at the wrong time. I'll tell you sometime if we can put up with each other. Saw your tale of woe on the national news, Spud. COOL name. Do you prefer mashed or baked? Ha, ha. I've been visiting you ever since you got out of the hospital. Some sense of humor you have. Your antics are out of this world." Her voice shook with the effort of not breaking out in laughter while speaking.

"Hey, slow down, woman. You talk faster than I can think, and I think pretty fast." Spud was having major problems keeping up the pace. He probably should stop staring at her chest.

She responded, speaking slowly, "OK, sorry, don't get much practice."

He questioned, "How can you become invisible?"

"You can do it too. I'm not really invisible. You just tell all the minds around you that you aren't there. It's real simple." She sounded confident.

"Yeah sure, for you maybe!" He sounded much less than confident.

"I can teach you...if you don't mind the way I look." Her voice took on a pitiful tone.

It took Spud milliseconds to reach a decision. This girl was the answer to an itch that he couldn't even admit he had, let alone scratch. He was so lonely it was pathetic, and besides, he sensed that she was in the same boat.

Bernard surprised him so much that he flinched. "She's OK! I like her! Don't do anything to mess this up, or I'm taking over, and that's a promise."

Bernard's threat was as ludicrous as it was out of character, but Spud promised him that he would be careful.

Bernard's last comment was, "You'd better be!"

Spud got back to his conversation with Constance. "Hey, I think we kind of go together. Besides, I'm working on fixing my looks. I grew my own fingers so—"

She interrupted, "I've been trying for a lot longer than you and all I can do is convince people that I look different."

"Yeah well, I'm not giving up. Besides, maybe we aren't capable of doing the same things. We are, after all, entirely different people with entirely different brains and entirely different injuries. The odds would be astronomical if we were the same past certain points. It boggles my mind that there are two of us this similar. After graduation, I'm going to see a friend in prison and then away somewhere and...well...maybe we could go together?"

His answer caused her to think before she responded. "Why worry about graduating? Kind of silly when you could ace any college exam ever written after spending ten minutes reading the appropriate book."

He had been thinking of this for a considerable time. "I have some things to take care of at graduation!"

"OK, mind if I tag along. I'm tired of being by myself, and stalking you invisibly is getting tougher and tougher. Some of the stunts you have pulled are so funny I can barely control myself. Invisible people can't laugh out loud, you know, if they want to stay invisible anyway!" she responded.

"OK, let's go. Ah... mind staying in my apartment with me?" Spud nervously awaited her reply, and it was absolutely startling.

She spoke, sporting a huge grin. "Nope. Actually, I moved in a few days ago. Been sleeping on your couch. Oh, by the way, real nice butt!"

Spud spurted, "You're kidding? You saw me naked?"

All Spud got in response was laughter. Things were looking up. Maybe there was a little more to life than revenge. Payback Incorporated had looked promising, but maybe he'd become a master criminal or a politician. Wait a minute, those two careers were exactly the same except for politicians usually stole more money and had better retirement benefits.

Maybe Zippo could give him some advice. So many choices, so many decisions, and only one lifetime to do them in. Well, he'd have to see what could be done about that limitation also. Now that he had some help, who knows what could be accomplished! Hey! Maybe a crime-fighting duo! Or may—.

Bernard popped up with, "Yeah, with a big U on your shirts."

Spud knew better than to ask but did anyway. "Why a U?"

"For ugly and uglier," Bernard said, snickering so much he had trouble getting the words out.

Spud asked, "I thought you liked Constance?"

"I do. For me! Not you! What could a girl like her see in a killer like you?" Bernard screamed. "You're stronger than I am, but I'll get you. One of these days, I'll take over. You hear me? I'll get you!"

Spud was surprised. After Bernard's voice had receded, he started thinking about how he would like to kick Bernard in the head. They might not be the best-looking couple in the world, but being the smartest and coolest wasn't all that bad of a start. Besides, he wasn't really a killer, justice sometimes demanded more than just an ear be removed. Spud had the feeling that Constance would understand, maybe she had even settled some scores of her own on occasion, and if not, he would volunteer his aid. He would talk to her tonight after dinner.

Constance's voice interrupted his thoughts. "What are you thinking about, Spud?"

Spud's answer surprised even him. "Oh, I have a problem named Bernard to take care of. No big thing."

Bernard was wailing at the top of his lungs as Spud locked the door to his cell, so deep in his mind that Spud wasn't sure even he could ever find it again. Life would be a little strange without Bernard, but Spud was sure he could get by with a little help from a friend. Life sure throws you some curves. Some wearing tight sweaters and pants, some not. Luckily, Spud could catch anything tossed in his direction! And he knew what to do with it after he made the catch. HE AND CONSTANCE WERE ABOUT TO CHANGE THE WORLD!

To The Peculiar Ones

A special thank you to H.R. Shavor for the dedication poem "His Stories."

I want to acknowledge the hard work, effort, support, diligence, and knowledge of my two friends—Toni and Matthew. After my wife passed away, the dynamic duo went out of their way to support me and help me in any way they could. Without their constant support, this manuscript would have gone up in smoke, and my appreciation has no bounds. I will appreciate their friendship until my dying day! THANK YOU FOREVER, Toni and Matt!!!!!

About the author

Kenneth W. Hummell is a surly old man from the Vietnam War era who is loved by his friends. The old saying "been there, done that, got the t-shirt" describes Kenneth's full life. From the Pennsylvania mountains of his childhood to flying above the jungles of Vietnam on a Huey gunship, taming the metal steeds of a West Coast biker community, building race cars with some of the best, and most importantly, loving his wife, Jo. Every fictional story starts with a tidbit of reality. Kenneth's extraordinary reality lives anew in his stories, which he brings to life for you, the reader. So, enjoy this variety of odd stories that are just "A Little Further Off".